IMMORTAL SOULLESS: RESURRECTION

TANITH FROST

SPARROWCAT PRESS

Resurrection/ Tanith Frost

First edition, June 2017

For Kathy

Not all heroes have fangs. Thanks for being one of mine.

CHAPTER ONE

The faithful file into their little white church for the Easter Sunday evening service, oblivious to my huddled presence on the peaked roof across the street. Spring arrives late here in Newfoundland, and their breath is coming out in pale, smoky plumes like the sharply scented wood smoke billowing into the darkening sky from the brick chimney behind me.

When I was a kid, I pretended I was a dragon on days like this.

I draw cold air into my lungs, puffing up so that my leather jacket crushes my breasts, and hold it for a moment. When I force it back out, I can't see my breath. One needs significant body heat for a trick like that. Shame. That used to be fun.

God. How long has it been since I've let myself think of those days? We're not supposed to remember our lives, so I do my best to forget. A vampire is a vampire. A new creature, not a former... whatever. My childhood dreams, my school, my own little white church, my death. None of it matters now, and I've come a long way in letting go. But watching the people below me is making it hard not to remember.

The wind whips off the harbour behind me, tossing my bright blonde hair into a tangled mess in front of my face. I grab it in both hands and shove it under my grey scarf, then reach down to fiddle with the strings on my ripped jeans.

I should get out of the wind soon. Trixie will be looking for me. I haven't seen her since late this afternoon, when we woke and left the inn without eating. Our former hosts have no idea how grateful they should be that my sister trainee and I weren't hungrier.

Those people will never know what slept under their roof the past few days. We look like living people, though perfected versions of our own genetic potential, and hide our differences well. Direct sunlight burns our skin and eyes, but we can venture out in the early morning or evening on cloudy, foggy days—which Newfoundland provides in abundance—as long as we put on protective creams and sunglasses and stick to the shadows. Thanks to our training, Trixie and I have learned to breathe and blink at a normal pace when we're around the living. We speak carefully and keep a straight face so that no one sees our fangs.

That's not to say we ever socialize with the living, but we know all too well how essential it is that we blend in. We must remain invisible should we ever find ourselves among them.

And now we've proved we can. The two of us have been in training for over a year, becoming proficient at all of the basics. That doesn't make us tame monsters, but at least we're well controlled ones. This five-day vacation was a chance for us to test ourselves away from the protections and restraints of our trainer and our clan. I think we passed, but it hasn't been easy.

I adjust my sunglasses and settle my back against the warmth of the chimney as they close the church doors. The sky is overcast and the sun is quickly setting behind the clouds, but I hug the shadows. Even this light is too bright for my night-attuned eyes, and my skin has been tingling, warning me that this is not my place or my time. I belong to the night now, and this feels like cheating.

But it feels good to be out during the day for once, even if I can't feel the sun on my skin. To remember, though it sends a sickly wave of guilt through me when I do.

The electronic speakers in the church's bell tower, which have been calling the faithful to worship through the overpowering melody of clanging bluegrass hymns, change their tune. Now the entire neighbourhood has no choice but to enjoy the congregation's decidedly mixed vocal talents. I wince, but hold my place in spite of the racket.

They mean well. And it means something to them. Something I miss almost as much as my heartbeat if I let myself think about it too often.

I try not to. As it turns out, all of it—spirituality, the comfort of prayer, uplifting worship—was never really mine. I was born to become a creature of the night and the void. If I still feel a connection aching in my chest as the strains of Amazing Grace ring out, it's an illusion. Maybe it always was. I'll never know what would have awaited me on the other side of death if I'd been allowed to slip away.

Soft footsteps scrape over the rough shingles behind me. I don't turn. Instead, I keep my eyes on the blue minivan with rusted side panels that races up the street, swerving into the school parking lot a few doors down from the church.

Trixie plops herself down beside me and stretches her combat-boot-clad feet out in front of her, sprawling like a ragdoll. She stretches her pale fingers over the roof between her slim, lycra-covered thighs and leans forward to see what I'm looking at.

"What's happening, Aviva my dear?"

"Easter service."

"Jesus Christ." She wrinkles her pretty little nose, then rummages in her pocket and pops a piece of gum into her mouth.

I'm not sure whether she's cursing or making conversation. "I feel a certain affinity for him this time of year," I say, allowing a sardonic note to enter my voice. "Death. Coming back. Legions of unbelievers."

She nods, and her candy-floss pink pigtails bounce on her shoulders. I told her not to bleach and dye it last night, but it actually looks pretty cute. "Fluffy bunnies and chocolate. I hear you."

"That, too."

I squint at the cross on top of the steeple. So much more tasteful than the crucifix on display at the far quieter Catholic church down the road, but both symbols seem strange to me now. I was killed by an asshole with a gun. If I had followers, I sure as hell wouldn't want them wearing pistols on gold chains around their necks.

Maybe I never understood it properly. Too late to ask now. Questions have a habit of getting me in trouble, anyway.

And I don't care. I really don't.

Trixie lifts her sunglasses and narrows her exquisite green eyes at the family that piled out of the minivan, who are now approaching the broad front steps of the church. The mom is juggling a baby in a car seat, a massive diaper bag, her purse, and several coats. No wonder her lipstick is smudged and her slip is showing below the hem of her shapeless dress. I'm impressed she managed to get her shit together enough to almost make it to the evening service on time.

Trixie clucks her tongue. "Shameful tardiness. Lines must've been long at Walmart."

I don't answer. The dad is coming, taking long, purposeful strides. A little girl trails behind him. New dress for Easter. No question. She's the most cheerful thing in this bleak springtime landscape, all blonde hair and pink cheeks and bright floral dress. Sleeveless. She must be freezing, but likely didn't want to cover up her pretty clothes. She stops at the bottom of the steps to twirl, giggling as her skirt flares out in a tidy bell shape around her legs.

A living person wouldn't hear the laugh or see the details that I do at this distance. Even with my senses dulled after almost a week without feeding, I catch all of it.

"Mommy, look!" she calls.

But Mom is gone. Dad hears and thunders back down the steps, grabbing the girl by her upper arm. His fingers dig into her flesh as he leans in to hiss something in her ear. Her chin trembles, but she nods and follows him into the church.

I don't realize I've bared my fangs until Trixie pokes me in the ribs, pulling me out of my hyper-focused outrage.

"Forget them. Assholes happen, remember? Even in the best neighbourhoods." She glances back over her shoulder, taking in the dull water of the harbour, the laughable grocery store beside the school, the dead grass of the yard below. "And this ain't one of the best."

"You don't have to remind me. I knew plenty of those assholes in my time."

I'm trying to shake it off. The living are supposed to mean nothing to us. Even the families we left behind. I guess I'm lucky that I left just a grandmother and a sister to mourn me. I managed to make it past my teen years without a spouse or a kid hanging off me, and I'd already lost my closest friends before my death. It's made it a little easier to cut ties to the life I lost. To distance myself from my past.

But this fucker grabbing his kid is pissing me off. If I had a heartbeat it would be racing right now, sending adrenaline coursing through my system, making me do something stupid.

Instead I lean back on my elbows. "Guess our vacation must be almost over."

"Just what I was going to say. And here you are, wasting our last moments of precious, glorious freedom mooning over useless people we can't even feed on. Get your ass up. I want to get out of here before Daniel tracks us down and makes us get back to work."

The sound of a throat clearing rumbles behind us, and Trixie winces.

"How unfortunate that you've missed your opportunity," Daniel drawls. His voice comes closer, but I don't hear his footsteps. That's chilling enough, but it's worse that I don't *feel* him coming. I can often sense Trixie before I see her, and I should know Daniel almost as well by now. He's been training the two of us in basic skills ever since he was assigned the thankless task of shaping two new vampires released from the acclimation facility. Teaching us to fight. To fall. Kicking our asses every day until we learned to ignore the pain.

Showing us how to keep the secret of our existence. Demanding that we control our appetites and feed in approved locations without killing.

A deep ache spreads through me at the thought of feeding. Much as it's been nice to have a few days off, to have time and freedom to race at top speed across rocky meadows and over pebbled beaches, to scent the night wind and experience the world without Daniel breathing down our necks, judging every action... I'm starving. I'd be lying if I said it hadn't been hard spending the past few nights in that little inn with living, breathing humans under the roof, their pulses calling to me like a love song.

My mouth waters, filling with the sharpness of the mild poison that enters our victims when we feed. Stock, we call them. The hopeless addicts who return again and again to offer us their blood. The taste of my own venom makes me feel half alive. Awake. More aware than I've felt since we left the city and the possibility of feeding. It's like lust, but so much deeper than what any living person will ever experience.

And satisfying that lust...

I force my thoughts away from that. There's no one here we can feed on. I understand now why no vampires live in these pretty little towns. These places might have been tempting for a stopover back when lone vampires could hunt and feed at will. But now St. John's is where the stock gather, where we give them the illusion of safety and the promise of pleasure in exchange for their precious blood.

Daniel steps in front of us and crosses his arms. He's almost too gorgeous, even for a vampire. He'd look like a stereotypical surfer dude if he wasn't so pale. Broad-shouldered and strong-jawed, with killer cheekbones and this thick brown hair that refuses to behave—which I imagine drove him crazy when he was alive, back in the days of slicked down styles and swing music. He looks fantastic, strong and rested. A few days away from us has agreed with him.

"You need to learn to hide your thoughts better, Aviva." A smirk spreads across the chiseled features beneath the reflective aviator shades that cover his cold hazel eyes. His voice is rich. Not chilling like the scary monster-type vampire from the movies. Not douchey like the teen heartthrob ones. Deep. Warm. "A fellow might get the wrong idea from the expression on your face."

I sneer up at him, but it's half-hearted. I leave the mouthing off to Trixie. She's better at it than I am. I care too much about doing well, about pleasing my trainer. An unfortunate holdover from who I was when I lived.

Good girl. Teacher's pet.

The irony of it is that I'd be far better off with Trixie's attitude. She's a pain in Daniel's finely shaped ass, no doubt, but her devil-may-care personality lets her take risks and let go of the past. She's taken to unlife as a vampire like the proverbial duck to water.

And if we're being honest and sticking with metaphors, I'm the fish that's struggling to breathe on land.

Daniel frowns at Trixie's pink hair. "Beatrix, really."

She purses her lips and stares up innocently in spite of his disappointed dad tone. "What?"

"Should I assume that this is another room deposit I won't be getting back, or did you manage to clean up after yourself?" He learned a year ago that there's no point yelling at her, but there's nothing pleasant in his tone.

Trixie tilts her head at him and sighs. "Well, Daniel, if you would release us from training and let us have real jobs, it would be *me* not getting the deposit back."

"I would if I could. Believe me."

Trixie blows a massive bubble that matches her new hair colour and pulls it back into her mouth with a loud smack. "Then I guess we're all stuck, aren't we?"

Daniel casts a long-suffering glance up at the clouds,

and I try not to laugh. He's not so bad, really. Terrifying at first. Cold. Deadly attractive, but with a predatory look in his eyes that never leaves, even when he seems like he's relaxed. He trains us like he's trying to prove something, even though it's the last thing he wants to be doing. It's not a labour of love for our Daniel. He used to have a more important job in clan law enforcement, but he's never told us how he ended up sheltering our sorry asses under his roof for the past year.

Maybe I'll ask him. Some day. In another eighty years or so, when I've been dead as long has he has now.

Despite everything, he's a good trainer. I'd be too easy on my students. Too soft. Too understanding when their newly turned bodies objected to the torture I put them through. Too encouraging even when they failed.

I once wished for understanding. An occasional "good try" when I fucked up a sparring match. I wanted to be coddled. Respected.

Like a living human.

Now? Now I'm ready to get back to work. The fact is that in this new world I exist in, you earn respect. You don't get it just for showing up. And if Daniel is hard enough on me that I hate him sometimes, if he yells back when I scream at him, if he breaks me down and demands that I do the hard work of building myself back up so that I know how to stand on my own... That's the only way I'm going to survive.

I don't like it, but I'm learning to appreciate it.

Sort of.

Getting some distance from him has probably helped. I'm sure I'll hate him again tomorrow.

"We going back?" I ask, not sounding like it matters. We're supposed to be working on patience and presence, accepting what comes. We have hundreds of years ahead of us. More, if we're lucky. No need to be in a rush.

"Vacation is over," he tells us. "You'll have to leave this community to its—what in the name of the void is this racket?"

The speakers, which were turned off during the speaking parts of the service, have interrupted Daniel with a fresh wave of song.

He shakes his head and winces as a sharp soprano overwhelms the rest of the choir. "I remember when church music was at least pleasant, if you had to put up with it at all. Do people around here actually tolerate caterwauling carolers every week without complaint?"

"Carols are for Christmas," I remind him.

"As if it mattered." He glares down at me, sending a chill down my spine even though I can't see his eyes. I remind myself, not for the first time, that it's not attraction I feel when he gives me that look, but fear. Daniel could chain me up and hang me by my ankles from a rooftop in the sunrise if he wanted to teach me a lesson, and no one would step in.

He wouldn't. But as my trainer, he could. That's not attractive, no matter how nice he is to look at. Or it shouldn't be.

I look away, back toward the street.

"We're needed in town," he says, watching as we continue to laze on the shingles. "Though it doesn't look like either of you are ready for your first assignment."

We're both on our feet before the last word is out of his mouth. Trixie spits her wad of gum in a graceful arc over the edge of the roof. "What is it?" she asks, and now she sounds attentive. Eager.

We've been waiting for this. Responsibility. A chance to prove ourselves worthy of complete freedom, to make our mark and find our places within Maelstrom, the clan we've sworn loyalty to.

My stomach knots, but I don't let it show on my face.

"I told Miranda weeks ago that you're ready. She needs me to return to my old position for a time, and she requested that I bring you to the club tonight so she can meet you and judge for herself."

My mouth dries up. I'm sure I imagined the emphasis on the word judge, but there it is. Another chance to fail.

I won't. I *am* ready.

Daniel rakes his hand through his unruly hair again. "Get in the car. I'm taking you home." He turns away, but pauses midstep. "And ladies? If you disappoint me, your young, dead asses are mine. You will not embarrass me tonight. Understood?"

Trixie grins at me and lets out a restrained squeal. I bounce on the toes of my boots, allowing excitement to grow in me for the first time since I can remember.

He thinks we're ready. Both of us, not just Trixie. The past year of training is about to pay off. We're going to take our places. Learn the secrets of vampire life that have been forbidden until we proved ourselves worthy. Earn our keep, move up in the clan.

I haven't had a choice about being a vampire. Not since someone chose to turn me after my unfortunate and early death. Accepting my fate has been hard. This is my chance to embrace it, once and for all.

"So what's the assignment?" Trixie asks.

Daniel looks back. "Rogues." He disappears off the edge of the roof without another word.

As if one were needed.

My newfound energy seems to flow back out through the flat soles of my boots, leaving me empty and weak-kneed. Trixie glances at me, chewing her lip. "On our first assignment?" she whispers.

We've always known that Daniel used to hunt rogue vampires— those who continued in the old ways instead of feeding on approved stock. Killers. Monsters who threatened to expose our existence with every unwilling body they left behind. But they haven't been around for so long. Not here, anyway.

"Are you two coming or not?" Daniel doesn't have to yell. We're listening. We hear. "Your choice. If you're ready, that is."

His black beast of a car roars to life just down the street.

We hesitate for a second, then Trixie flashes her fangs in a wide grin and grabs my hand.

We hit the ground running.

CHAPTER TWO

E ven at the speeds Daniel drives, it takes us five
hours to get back to St. John's.

The glow of the city appears long before we
can see the buildings themselves. Intense light pollution
for such a small city, but this place is full of contradictions.

At times it feels like a small town, especially when I
walk the streets of downtown late at night, peering in the
windows of shops selling hand-knitted wool mittens, non-
fiction and local interest books, and partridgeberry jam made
in-province. It's unashamed of its age, flaunting its history up
and down the streets that hug the harbour. There's a histor-
ical plaque on every corner, I'd swear to it. The sidewalks are
shadowed by towering churches built in a neo-gothic style
that's technically a copycat of European cathedrals, but
they're so old themselves that it doesn't seem to matter.

Those are the parts of the city that make me wish I'd discovered it when I was alive. When I could enter those churches, when I could visit those shops and speak with the owners. When it was okay for me to be interested in humanity.

The rest of it—the new parts, the shiny parts, the parts built on oil money after the cod fishery collapsed—are the bits I care less for, and sadly, we're heading right through them. We've taken an unfamiliar route tonight due to construction, one that takes us up through the newest of the new shopping districts. Bright neon advertising signs. The empty hulk of an American department store that existed in Canada for about five minutes.

We pass a group of young people exiting one of the fancy coffee shops that mirror each other on either side of the road. The women wear high boots with precarious looking heels. The men laugh, and one punches another on the arm.

So little has changed since I died, yet I feel more of a connection with the old parts of this city than the new. Maybe it's the creeping understanding that these people walking the streets are blips, momentary inhabitants who aren't likely to have a lasting impact on their world. Trixie and Daniel and I... we will become as ancient as this city herself if we play our cards right.

And tonight, I reflect as we turn onto Torbay Road and

shoot toward downtown, we might play a small part in saving those blips.

I'm trying to focus on that instead of the meeting that lies in my immediate future. Miranda. I've never met her, but I've heard stories about her. She's not the oldest vampire around, but she's ancient and active enough to be called a true elder, the most powerful one in our clan. She's seen centuries pass, seen younger vampires come and go. She was instrumental in the creation of the society most vampires now live in and the rules we all adhere to in spite of the differences between clans.

We pledged loyalty to Maelstrom, but that was the same as offering it to Miranda. If we had a queen, she would be it.

And she wishes to judge me on what seems to me a rather shaky record.

I feel ill.

Trixie leans forward. "Are we there yet?"

No one answers.

Trixie's been exiled to the backseat ever since she took Daniel's old GTO out for a midnight joyride after a particularly good feeding and totalled it. The Challenger is a fine replacement as far as I'm concerned, but Daniel still seems bitter. Though technically her sentence is up, I think she sticks to the back in the interest of self-preservation.

Smart girl.

We leave the glow of the upper city behind and enter

the tree-shadowed streets of downtown. My mouth waters at the thought of the club being just minutes away. My hunger's actually a welcome distraction now, and it's all I can do not to bolt from the car when Daniel parks. I leave my jacket and scarf behind. We'll be warm and comfortable soon enough.

The Inferno is the best-kept secret in St. John's. The owner's name is Dante. He thinks the club's name is terribly clever, but otherwise he isn't a bad guy. Human, of course. Present during the day, paying taxes on the meagre income he declares. Everything is aboveboard at this little hole-in-the-wall bar nestled in a dark downtown alley, at least as far as the living are concerned.

The battered, graffiti-covered door looks like it should creak when Daniel leans his forearm against it and pushes, but it swings open on silent hinges. The room beyond is dim, lit by electric lights shaded in red glass to cut the glare. I tuck the arm of my sunglasses, which I had been wearing to shield against the bright streetlights uptown, into the low-cut V of my top. Daniel slips his into his pocket, looks back to make sure Trixie and I are following, then steps briskly toward the bartender.

No living humans have wandered in to the bar tonight. Every one of the rickety moisture-stained tables is unoccupied, just as they should be. No need to act casual.

The rules still stand, though.

"Get you something?" the bartender asks. Dante's not

working, but this one looks familiar. It's almost scary how alike they're all starting to look to me, these interchange-able bartenders in their white shirts and dark vests, standing there polishing their martini glasses and looking like something out of an old movie.

"Is she in?"

Daniel is testing him, but the bartender—a living human—doesn't break a sweat under that cold stare. I step closer and lean on the bar.

"Not sure what you mean," the bartender says, setting the clean glass down and picking up another that doesn't really need polishing. It's a rare night that a single drink gets poured up here. The Inferno's reputation among the living is one star at best.

Daniel grins, and his elongated canine teeth reflect the dim light. "Good thing you don't. I'll have something warm. And red."

Not that there's any doubt about what Daniel is, but the password is protocol. Everything is regimented. It wasn't always this way. Vampires once lived (or rather, didn't live) in solitude, responsible for managing their own territories. But after the hunts and purges centuries ago that nearly annihilated our population, they began to understand the need for unity, for a new way of existing that would allow us to remain secret.

I still don't know half of what it all means. But I'll

learn. I already know more than this guy, who probably feels important up here, guarding the door.

The human bartender holds Daniel's gaze for a moment, then reaches under the bar to flip a switch. Daniel turns away without acknowledging the action and pushes through a crimson velvet curtain to our right. Trixie pauses to wink at the bartender and run her tongue over her fangs, and I hang back, enjoying his valiant attempt to appear disinterested.

The living can be so much fun.

A low growl from Daniel sends us scurrying after him down a tight spiral staircase. It's nearly pitch black in here, but that's not a problem for us.

It feels like descending into a grave.

It feels like coming home.

I still find it hard to label some of my feelings now that I lack some of the automatic physical sensations that come with them. When I lived, I assumed that my body responded to my feelings. Now, I'm not sure. I can't read myself anymore. I know I'm anxious, but without a racing heartbeat to confirm it, it feels less real.

I suppose it's natural to be nervous at a time like this, but there's not much that's natural about me anymore.

There are times when my human life seems like ancient history. When I realize that all of the songs I like came out before I died, or when I feel like smacking teenagers in books for bitching about petty adolescent problems that matter so little in the grander scheme of life and death. Or when I'm feeding, feeling the strength and power of human blood coursing through me like I've tapped into the very essence of life itself. I've only been a vampire for a few years, but in those moments I can almost forget I was once one of them.

Other times, like tonight, I'm terribly aware of how new I am. How fragile and untested, how isolated I've been during my year of training and my adjustment period before that. Even Daniel, who's been dead since before my grandparents were born, who's quickly recognized by the bouncer lurking at the bottom of the stairs and nodded through another curtain... even he's relatively new. Not even a century dead.

The bouncer, a massive fellow with skin and clothing so dark he could be the night itself, narrows his pale golden eyes at me and Trixie as we pass by after Daniel. Evaluating. Those eyes would have been brown when he lived, but they've paled with death. He's new, too. They'll get darker as he ages.

I know the foggy grey of my eyes gives my own youth away. Wisps of cloud, Trixie called them when we met, her pale emerald irises sparkling with her impish grin. What would I have done without her humour to pull me out of my post-death melancholy? I doubt I'd have survived the recovery facility.

I was a hard case right from the start, no question. It's a wonder Daniel took me on.

It's still dark beyond the curtain, but brighter than the stairwell, lit with dim incandescent bulbs under coloured shades. It's comfortable for both vampires and the humans who mill about, drinks in hand. Watching. Posing. Flirting. Low, hypnotic music hums through hidden speakers. Vampires approach the bar, making careful selections and swiping payment cards as the living watch with barely concealed interest.

The volume of stock here tonight confuses me until I remember that tomorrow is a holiday. They're all squeezing one last thrill into their long weekend, knowing they'll feel a bit drained and sluggish tomorrow. They stand in small groups, laughing, swaying to the music.

Daniel motions for me to wait, then takes Trixie through a door that blends almost seamlessly into the wall. I'm fine with him taking her to Miranda first.

I need to get rid of my nerves, but it's hard to calm myself when controlling my breath isn't an option. Instead I hug the wall and watch the crowd.

A copper-skinned male vampire I don't know personally but have seen around the club before approaches a blonde woman. She's middle-aged and fit, wearing a miniskirt and a top that shows off her toned stomach. We don't really care about what they wear, but they do like to show off for each other. To make it a special occasion.

Bless them.

What's caught his attention, I suspect, is not her towering heels or long legs, but the blood-red ribbon she's tied around her neck with a jaunty bow at the back, accenting her most appealing feature. The vampire takes her hand and whispers something into her ear. She giggles and nods, then tilts her head to one side. Questioning.

He produces a clear vial filled with bright yellow liquid, purchased from our end of the bar. She studies it, bites her lip, then nods again, more eagerly. There's nothing coy about this one. There rarely is when we offer the good stuff. He empties the vial into her wine glass, and she swirls it into the drink.

She's done this before. The new ones are always uncertain and sloppy.

My mouth waters again. Many of the other humans look on, some smiling, some clearly envious. The blonde finishes her wine in one gulp, and a grin spreads slowly across her face. Her teeth are terrible, her face careworn, but the joy that radiates from her makes her a thing of true beauty. She laughs and leans on her temporary master's arm as he leads her to an alcove and closes the curtains.

That little transaction took less than a minute, but he'll have as much time as he wants to enjoy her in private. It will be good for her. The vials, each filled with a drug designed to induce a specific emotion in our stock humans, are a lovely draw for them, and offer a customized experience for us. But that's not what keeps them coming back. Our venom does that. Mildly intoxicating, entirely addictive.

They don't stand much chance of not returning. Not if we want them to.

As the minutes pass, I grow less nervous about my meeting and more concerned about my dwindling options for feeding. It's early yet, but I'd like to get on with it before all that's left are the used-up humans who come too frequently. Dull. Lifeless. I need something strong tonight if I'm to be at my best.

"Aviva?"

Daniel has reappeared. I glance around for Trixie. There. She's already got a vial in her hand, but it's no bright yellow serum. The vial is clear, but the liquid within is dark and cloudy, swirling with black flecks. Just looking at it gives me chills.

I don't understand why we'd want the stock to feel fear or sadness before we feed. I can't imagine it would be fortifying in and of itself. And carrying a black vial ensures that the dregs are all we get, unless someone newer is feeling truly adventurous. The used-up ones are desperate enough to subject themselves to any pain just to get their fix.

I silently wish Trixie luck and follow Daniel toward the same door he took Trixie through. He turns back and gives me a look like he wants to say something, but he decides against it, and his expression clears as he opens the door for me.

I wonder what happens if I don't pass inspection. It's too late to ask now, and I wouldn't even if I could.

Save face. Look calm.

I try not to let my boots clomp as Daniel leads me to whatever awaits behind the door at the end of the long hallway.

CHAPTER THREE

I've never gone this deep before.

The rooms that line this hallway are used for purposes I haven't been introduced to. Meetings. Deciding of fates. God knows what else.

Daniel pauses outside the door at the end and knocks. Its whiteness stands in stark contrast with the dark walls and the dark paint on the other doors. There's no nameplate. Miranda doesn't need one.

I've never met her, yet I feel the chill of her presence as we approach. She's not hiding herself from me.

I wonder whether she knows how intimidating that is.

Though there's no answer from inside the room, Daniel opens the door and stands aside. I glance up at him, but his face remains blank as I enter. No encouragement. No slap on the ass and *try your best*. I'm on my own.

Elegant is the first word that comes to mind when I

enter the room. It's not comfortable, but it's less grim than I expected from an elder. I'd heard that older vampires all slept in coffins and preferred the haunted mansion aesthetic, but this room is... I can't place it. A Victorian flavour with a dash of Wild West brothel thrown in for good measure, all dark wood, overstuffed chairs, ruffles, and a little more lace than seems proper. But I like it. Or I would if I wasn't fucking terrified.

I turn my head slowly toward the corner, toward the source of the undeniable power that's prickling over my skin like electricity.

Miranda.

She's far more interesting than the room's contents. Tall and pale, wearing a floor-length white dress with lace trim that comes up high at the front and low at her wrists. Her midnight hair is swept up in an intricate twist at the back of her head, revealing a graceful neck that's arched like the stem of a lily as she looks down at the leather file folder in her hand.

It's all paperwork for us. Electronic screens are too bothersome for our sensitive eyes. More than that, this is how it's always been done. Tradition is everything.

I take a step toward her, then freeze as she looks up.

Her eyes are black, or as close to it as blue can be.

"Aviva Siobhan Walker," she says as she steps toward me, weaving her way around a spindle-legged wooden table and stopping beside a heavy desk that's set out from the wall, facing into the room. Her eyes meet mine. "Pretty name."

"Thank you. I liked it."

I haven't heard my full name since I died. My parents called me by my middle name when I was alive, and my mother always shrugged when I asked why they didn't just name me Siobhan. Or why she wouldn't let me go by Aviva, which would have been so much easier to pronounce. If I'd heard *sy-oh-bah-hawn* from an annoying classmate or substitute teacher one more time, I might have lost my mind.

At least in death, I was allowed to name myself. It offered a necessary degree of separation from my living self, but I didn't stray far. I wasn't ready to.

Miranda smiles gently, as though she understands. She could be reading my mind, if that's her particular gift. I can't tell. Everything about her is so overpowering that I doubt I'd notice if she were hypnotizing me.

She glances at the papers in the file again. "Just twenty years living." She clucks her tongue softly. "Origin of transformation blood factor unestablished, both parents predeceased, no family history of vampirism. Cause of death, gunshot to the..." She flips the page. "Abdomen. Correct?"

I nod. For a group of beings who are supposed to forget our pasts, we certainly seem to keep excellent records of them.

"Tea?" she asks, setting the file on the desk. I suspect

she's memorized its contents already, but is making a show of needing the records for my sake. She glides to a lace-frosted table next to the back wall, where a silver tea set awaits. I nod, but I'm not quite sure what to do. How to speak to her. I never asked.

Miranda gestures to a chair that looks like it belongs in a museum or period play, though I couldn't say which period. History was never my thing until I realized I was likely to be seeing a whole lot of it go by. I sit, and she hands me a steaming cup of Earl Grey. We don't eat solid food, but caffeine is the next best thing to blood as far as I'm concerned. I accept with thanks.

"You go by Aviva, then?"

"Usually. Trixie tends to call me Viva. I'm not sure whether she sees the irony."

Miranda chuckles into her teacup, closing her eyes so that her long, black lashes rest against her pale skin. "Viva la vampire."

I smile back for the first time. "Exactly. Ma'am."

"Miranda will be fine." She sets her cup down and leans back in her chair, studying me. Not unkindly, but a chill passes over my skin. God. Her *power*. I catch hints of it in myself sometimes, but not like this. No matter how fast I run, how high I jump, how feeding thrills me, I can't shake the feeling that there's more. That being a true vampire still lies on the other side of a locked door.

She clears her throat. "Daniel tells me your training is progressing well."

"Does he? He never says so to me." Though I suppose progress is relative. I started in a bad place.

"No, I'd say he wouldn't." She smiles warmly. She knows my trainer far better than I do. "Physical traits seem to be your strong suit. Dexterity, covert movement, strength, pain resistance, flexibility, all excellent as of his last report. Emotional state steady, particularly in recent months. Mental processes quick, extrasensory awareness average. Further skills thus far absent or not noted. Impressive progress, indeed. I know things were... difficult."

I've never heard someone call "average" impressive. For the first time, I realize that I have no idea what standard I'm being held up to. What is normal for a vampire two years dead, after one year of training? I only have Daniel's standards to judge by, and they've always been out of my reach.

"Thank you, ma'am. I mean, Miranda. Daniel is a good trainer. He's trying to help me with my perception issues, and we're still hoping I'll find deeper gifts." I should be grateful that that's all there is to work on besides whatever I need to learn on the job. Daniel's highly disciplined training style really has worked wonders.

"And you'll continue to work with him on that." She tilts her head slightly. "Tell me, does he seem to enjoy his current position?"

"Not in the least."

The corners of her eyes crinkle as she presses her lips together, suppressing a laugh. I think I like Miranda, terrifying though she is. It can't be easy to keep a sense of humour when you've seen as much of the world as she has. "As I suspected. Well, do take advantage of his expertise while you can, though I suspect he'll need his space during the investigation. You won't be taking an active role, but it will be a chance for you to hone your skills. Assist, observe, learn as much as you can. You'll have access to some of the best hunters in the field. Listen to them and do as they say."

This advice is unnecessary. I've already learned to respect authority, and every older vampire is in a position of authority over me right now. I lower my gaze and nod.

"You have great potential, Aviva, and we need all the help we can get right now."

Her admission surprises me. I've never seen so much as a crack in Maelstrom's perfect marble facade.

"It's rogues, right?" I say. I keep my expression even, but can't hold off the chill that passes over my already cool skin. It might be unfair to say I've never faced anything so dangerous. I have, after all, been murdered once before. But we civilized vampires are quite comfortable in the system we have set up, with our consensual feedings and victims who walk out of the club alive, if weak, when we're done with them. The rogues threaten everything my elders have worked for so long to establish.

I'm struggling to remember what I've learned about them, but I'm not coming up with much. They're savage. Cruel. They kill their victims and dump the bodies. They're often driven to it after committing crimes that get them banished from their clans, which means they have nowhere to feed legally. Banishment pushes them to crimes punishable by true death, and therefore oblivion.

It seems strange that we don't just execute them for their original crimes to prevent them going rogue, but I'm not about to question the wisdom of ancient creatures. Maybe on some level even monsters believe in redemption.

I'm hoping Miranda will fill in some blanks for me, but she merely pours more tea. "That is the issue, yes. Daniel will take you and Trixie to the crime scene tonight. Normally we'd leave it to more experienced hunters and let you two sit this one out, but we're a little short on help. Bram moved to Washington to assist with some quiet lobbying, and Katya has been in London on a diplomatic visit and hasn't returned yet. We need bright, observant minds on this. Daniel thinks you're ready. Would you say the same?"

I straighten in my chair. "Absolutely."

Bright minds. I had one when I was alive, even if I realize now that I wasted it. I have one still, and I know that I can use it to become so much better. I'm not great yet, but I could be. I can see it now.

And according to Miranda, Daniel sees it too. That shouldn't matter to me. In fact, he's probably hidden his approval because he knows I'd thrive on it. My need for outside validation could cost me greatly in this world.

Still, I can't help feeling better knowing I'm more ready than I realized.

Miranda's mouth quirks up at one corner. She is reading me. I know it.

"Any other questions?" she asks.

Of course. So many, and the most important ones have nothing to do with rogue vampires. I want to know why we are what we are, and more than that, who made me what I am. Who sensed the transformation factor in my blood before my death and changed me after. I'd wager that the answer to that last question is in that file on Miranda's desk, but I won't ask.

I can't let her see that I care.

"I think I can ask Daniel anything else. I don't want to take up any more of your time."

She chuckles, low and cold. "My dear, all I have is time. You'll understand that someday. But I imagine you're hungry."

I rise, eyes wide, as she touches a panel on the wall next to her that slides back, revealing dozens of vials in more shades and tones than I've ever seen, far beyond what living eyes would recognize. All clear, all in the same round, pointed-bottom shape, resting in rows of metal rings affixed to the wall. "Choose what you like."

I approach slowly, taking in the full array. In one sense, it doesn't matter. Blood is blood. But I'll take something from my victim's mood when I feed, and I want all the help I can get tonight.

Yellow will bring happiness, and the various shades might narrow that to joy, pleasure, ecstasy, contentment. Red enrages them—a challenge, and one that might be worth experiencing someday should I find a willing and worthy human to take it. We can't always predict the exact effect on an individual, but it's reasonably consistent.

I reach for a vial of nearly clear liquid, tinted slightly toward turquoise, and let my hand hover near the glass. I'm not sure what the colour means, but it feels right. I lift it gently by the neck and cradle it in one hand.

"Your friend has darker tastes," Miranda observes with a mysterious smile. The dark vials rest in the bottom row. I don't care to look at them.

"She always has. Thank you for this." We never see this kind of variety out on the club floor. This is the good stuff.

"Enjoy."

With her dismissal, my thoughts turn toward the club and the stock roaming the floor. My muscles tighten and my skin tingles as I stalk back up the hallway in long strides, and I become overly aware of the sharp length of my fangs.

All thoughts of rogues and questions about my origin fade from my mind, and the fact that Daniel hasn't waited to see how I made out barely registers. For now there is only the scent of blood filling the edges of my awareness, the throbbing heartbeats of the living, and a craving that pulls me far from any affinity with humanity.

Tonight, they are my prey.

CHAPTER FOUR

I spot my target immediately after I've slipped from the quiet hallway into the low, throbbing hum of the club floor. He's beautiful. Big and strong and hand-some, just a little rough around the edges, dressed in old jeans and a new white t-shirt that clings to his working guy muscles. Ears a tiny bit too big, brown hair a little shaggy, one tooth crooked when he casts a nervous grin over his shoulder. Just imperfect enough to be perfect. I suspect that even if I were still alive I'd be tempted to consume him whole.

The guy he's standing with says something, and he laughs a little. He drinks his whisky in short sips as his gaze wanders again, taking everything in. I hope it helps him relax. I want him, but it can wait a few minutes. No point pushing when he's on edge.

But I find it so hard to resist. It's the life in them that

sustains and strengthens us, and he's got more life in him than most of the stock here tonight. Something in him burns brighter than in his companions, warm and solid and so deliciously alive that it comes off him in waves, even from where I'm standing.

I can't remember the last time I needed blood this badly. Perhaps our vacation was a lesson to teach us to appreciate what will happen if we find ourselves cast out from vampire society and starving. That would be just like Daniel.

I take a half step closer and inhale.

This is why we only drink from live stock. They've tried banking in the past, but we waste away on a diet of harvested blood. Our brilliant scientists can do many things, but it seems there's no way to preserve or replicate the spark that feeds us. It has to come from the source. So we offer them a seemingly safe place to enjoy the pleasure of our poison.

The stock always seem to think the relationship is symbiotic. Really, we're more like keepers of a free-range flock. They mean no more to us than sheep or cattle.

Ideally. I've never seen a cow that looked this fuckable.

"Virgin," Daniel whispers in my ear. He's seen me watching, and I hear the smile in his voice. "I saw the blindfold when they brought him in."

"I'm not surprised. He's lovely."

"I saved him for you. Trixie wanted him, but I didn't

think her tastes would lead to him coming back any time soon."

"I'd say not. Thanks, boss."

I glance up at him, and he grins. He knows I've never had new blood before. "Watch yourself, there," he murmurs, and then he's gone.

My prey sees me coming and nearly drops his glass as he takes me in with wide eyes. "Shhhh," I whisper, locking his wandering gaze with my own. He smiles, and though there's still some nervousness there, he clearly likes what he sees in me. Petite frame. Decent tits shown off spectacularly in this shirt. Pretty face, flawless skin. Death does have its benefits.

I motion him closer, and he leans down so I can whisper in his ear. "You ready to have some fun?"

He pulls back and looks down at the vial in my hand. "Is that going to hurt me?"

"No, my love," I say, adopting the local pet name bestowed on friend and stranger alike. "If anything's going to hurt you, it'll be me. Only for a second, though." I smile slowly, revealing just the tiniest glimpse of fangs. "You'll love it."

He looks back at his friend, who grins and waves him off. I move with exaggerated, seductive grace toward an unoccupied alcove. My prey follows as though hypnotized by the sway of my hips, radiating excitement, fear, and life burning so bright and beautiful that I could cry.

Life. It's almost mine when I feed, but not quite. The great frustration of vampire existence, I suppose.

Before we step behind the curtains, I pour my vial into his drink. "Go ahead," I whisper. He can't hear it over the music, but he's watching my lips and gets the message. He only hesitates for a moment. Good boy. I love it when they follow orders.

His face goes blank. Then he smiles. "It's beautiful!" He looks down at me as though seeing me for the first time. "*You're* beautiful!"

I laugh and grab him by the front of his shirt. "Come on, big guy."

He follows willingly. His friend might have given him some idea of what to expect, but his friend's recollection will have been fuzzy, the exquisite pleasure being the only clear memory. Enough to keep him coming back until the addiction truly sets in.

I draw the curtains closed. It's black as a cave in the alcove now, and I make no move to turn on the lamp. I can see him well enough, though he's as good as blind. I push him gently down to sit on the leather-upholstered bench against the wall, and he holds his hands out in front of him. Searching. I could step into them, let him touch me. Instead, I sidestep his grasp and wait until there's room to move between his hands, then I sit on one of his thighs, perched side-saddle. He jumps in surprise, then smiles uncertainly.

"Relax," I whisper, letting my breath caress his ear. "You can touch. Mind your manners, now."

I want him to chill out. I don't need his nervousness affecting me later. I have more than enough of my own.

The drug works its way deeper into his mind, and his tension drains away. I didn't give him happiness, but something like it is moving through him. I chose well.

"That's it," I murmur, rubbing the back of his neck. "Just enjoy it."

He draws a quick breath as I graze the underside of his jaw with my nose, drawing in his scent. He's followed instructions well. He's clean, but didn't shower with strong soap right before coming to the club, and he wears no scented lotions or colognes. The smell is all human, and all him, whoever he is.

It's always different, and always fascinating.

He rests his back against the padded wall and finally seems to remember his hands. They roam freely over my body, gingerly at first, gently tracing the curves of my breasts. I press forward into his grasp, letting my body awaken. He grows bolder, lifting and grasping, lightly pinching my hardening nipples as I trace my tongue over that magical spot on his neck where his blood, his life, pumps so close to the surface. He groans and tries to kiss me, but I push his face away.

That could be pleasant, but it's not what I came for. And I don't want to mar his beautiful face if I lose control.

I'm so close to the edge now that I can imagine it happening.

He hooks one arm around my waist, pulling me closer as his other hand continues to explore, pulling in frustration at my belt before slipping under my shirt. He groans as he pulls my bra down and caresses the cool skin beneath. His skilled groping is distracting me from my mission, sending delightful tingling sensations shooting from my breasts down to the apex of my thighs. I let him continue as I press my body harder against his, kissing his neck down to his collar-bone, nibbling a little, teasing myself until it's unbearable.

I could have had him by now, but it's so much more satisfying to make it last.

His rapid, ragged breathing tells me that he's enjoying himself already. I trail my hand down over his chest, over the hard muscles of his stomach, lower. Just to be sure.

Hey, there.

I laugh softly in his ear. "You like that?"

He whimpers in response, and I spin around to face him, straddling him, grinding my pelvis against him. He groans. I can only imagine what he sounds like to any keen-eared vampire standing outside the alcove. Still, they won't judge. We enjoy them as we see fit, and it's certainly no worse than whatever Trixie might be up to in one of the soundproof rooms at the other end of the club.

My mouth finds his throat again. My lips are drawn to

its heat, to that thing that goes beyond physical senses and calls to something deeper within me.

His hands are warm, and it doesn't seem to bother him that I'm so much colder. Perhaps it excites him, as it does so many others. He pulls me closer and moves his hard body beneath me, and I wonder whether perhaps feeding couldn't wait just a few minutes longer. I've never had a living man while I fed from him. Haven't allowed myself this pleasure with anyone since I died.

Let Trixie have her pain. I'll take the pleasure. And to bite him as he came would be—

He moves his head to catch my lips with his own and thrusts his tongue past them, cutting off my thoughts. The shock of it makes him stop moving, but only for a moment. He's tasted the venom in my saliva, if only the faintest hint of it, and he wants more. Whatever skills he's acquired with his fragile human girlfriends seem to be forgotten now in his desperation to get closer to me.

My left canine scrapes the surface of his tongue. He gasps at the pain, but doesn't pull back.

Just a drop of blood. Less than that, even, but it's enough. Any thought of sex leaves me as the blood lust returns, washing away every other desire in a flood of red. I was right about him. This life, fresh and untouched, is like nothing I've ever tasted. There is nothing else. This is life. It is existence. It is everything.

I pull away before I can bite his tongue off. He'll never know how close I came.

He twists his fingers into my hair to hold on to me, but his strength is nothing compared with mine. I could snap his well-muscled neck if I wished, or pin him down and drain him dry. I wonder whether he understands that.

I can't wait any longer. I twist my fingers into his thick hair and tilt his head back, exposing his throat. I lower my mouth onto him again and press my fangs to his skin, savouring the resistance of that thin barrier. He cries out as I break through.

It hurts them. Every time.

And then my mouth is sealed over the twin wounds, drawing the blood from him. The sounds rising helplessly from him turn to soft gasps of wonder and disbelief as my poison overcomes the pain. His pulse is strong, and his hot blood flows easily down my throat.

The melancholy that plagued me earlier and the initial uncertainty that I felt in Miranda's office are gone. I am real, I am present, I am powerful. With his life entering me, I am a fucking goddess. There is nothing outside of this moment that matters.

It's only now that I realize why Daniel told me to be careful when drinking this virgin blood.

It's going to be very hard to stop.

CHAPTER FIVE

Trixie passes out in the back seat of the Challenger before we make it the few blocks out of downtown, and only stirs and stretches when Daniel pulls into the drive-through of her favourite local coffee shop. I roll down my window, enjoying the night air on my skin.

We're on our way to the crime scene now, a house in Kilbride. There will be bodies, though no one has chosen to share the details with me yet. I'm not too worried. It's not like I don't have experience with death.

"Little too much of the good stuff there, kid?" Daniel asks Trixie after he's ordered three black coffees.

She mumbles something mostly unintelligible that ends in the word "fine."

I feel better than I ever have after I've fed, even if the effect has already worn off somewhat. I still feel incredible, powerful. Back when I was feeding, I could swear I felt almost alive, just before my rational fear of punishment overcame my wild need to drain my lovely victim dry.

Trixie must have got it even better, though. She looks like she's been slapped in the face by a million orgasms simultaneously.

She'll definitely be fine.

"Did you feed, Daniel?" I don't really need to ask. His colour is good. He looks as bright as I feel, if wilder. He always gets that look after he feeds, and even though I know he'll never step out of line, I sometimes see something dark and daring under his veneer of civility.

I'd call it something roguish if that word didn't have the connotations it has for us.

"I did. Don't think that one will be back any time soon, though."

"She freaked out, did she?" I'm assuming it was a woman. He likes them small and female, as fragile as I used to be when I was alive.

The blood's the same, but the aesthetics do improve the experience.

Daniel waits until I have a sip of coffee in my mouth before he speaks. "No. She got clingy."

I spit my coffee straight out the window, pelting the side of the car with hot liquid. I try to control my laughter, and can't.

Daniel tries to frown at the mess, but he knows damn

well it's funny. Every so often we get a human who's been reading too much vampire romance, who gets a ridiculous crush on one of us and expects to be loved and protected because she's special or something. Usually a she, though not exclusively. They don't understand that to a vampire, they're animals. Entertaining and useful pets at best, to be enjoyed as we wish, and only to be protected because their safety benefits us.

"She started crying when I was done with her. Ran after me, begging to know my name. Cried about loving me." He at least has the good grace to seem embarrassed for her.

"She didn't know any better." I cast a quick glance at Daniel, taking in his refined, masculine features and the impressive shape of his body under his button-down shirt. Can't really blame her for her little crush, especially given what she would have been experiencing under his fangs.

"She should have," he says, more seriously. "She's been around for a while. Not like yours."

I smile contentedly and settle back into my seat. Mine didn't give me any trouble. I left him weak but quite satisfied with his experience, if his dopey smile was any indication. I hope he'll come back some day. His blood won't be as strong next time, especially if he feeds someone again too soon, but I wouldn't mind another taste. I might even follow through on that idea for making him really happy before the bite. That could be fun.

It doesn't pay to have regulars, though. Not if you want to avoid situations like what Daniel ran into tonight. When that happens, the club's enforcers have to clear the stock's memories of us. It leaves them shattered, disoriented, and depressed, knowing that they're missing something that runs as deep as their blood but not knowing what it is. It's an addiction, a deep craving, and they have no idea how to ease the ache.

Trixie rouses herself as we pull up in front of the house in Kilbride. Duplex, two storey, and both sides look quiet. It would be identical to the other houses on the street if not for its brick exterior—in contrast with the siding on the others—and the fact that it sits on a corner lot, giving it significantly more space on every side. We make our way silently up an uneven, paved driveway crisscrossed with deep cracks, past an empty garden and a dark front window with a sticker on it noting the name of a local company that does replacements.

Nice enough place. Nothing fancy.

Daniel leads us around back, where the low light from inside illuminates the deck. "Try not to get in the way," he orders us quietly. "Stand back, take it in, and notice anything you can. Details will be key, and you're our freshest eyes."

I pause on the bottom step. Something is holding me back, freezing my muscles. My chest tightens. I've changed my mind, I think.

Trixie glances back at me.

No. I'm doing this. They're just humans. Corpses, now. There's nothing in there to be afraid of. I force my legs to push me up the stairs, though it feels like I weigh four hundred pounds.

I smell the room before I see it, a nauseating mix of shit and dead blood. Though I don't need to draw breath except to speak, it still creeps its way up my nostrils and into my mind. Daniel's shoulders tense as he takes in the scene beyond the sliding glass doors, but he doesn't try to shield us from it. He nods hello to a few vampires who are already here as Trixie eagerly steps around him to get a better look.

Splashes of blood streak the floors and the walls, a good few reaching the white ceiling. My first thought is that the elders must be wrong about it being rogues. No vampire would be this careless. The blood is dead and congealed now, but not long ago, when it flowed, it would have been unthinkable to waste it.

I step around Daniel's broad form, and gag for the first time in years.

They haven't removed her yet. I might be familiar with death, but not like this.

A woman's naked body lies on a wooden kitchen table that's streaked with blood. Her hands and body are covered with it, too. And the soles of her feet, as though she was pushing against the table, struggling to escape even as they cut into her, spreading her blood beneath her in grotesque finger-paint patterns. But there's nowhere she could have gone. She's tied to the table with cheap bungee cords that dig into the flesh of her slightly overweight, stretch-marked middle.

Her lower arms are free, and her legs. She could fight, but she couldn't escape.

Bile rises in my throat, bitter with the taste of coffee. I push it back and focus. Details, Aviva. Details.

Her body is a mess of wounds. Bite marks everywhere, tearing apart my idea that vampires couldn't be this wasteful. There aren't just bites, either. Slash marks cover her skin, likely made by the kitchen knives that litter the laminate floor. She's missing a huge chunk of flesh from her lower abdomen and another from her left thigh. A glob of it, fatty and glistening, rests in a clear glass bowl on the counter next to the fruit bowl. A grotesque still-life.

Still-death, maybe.

God, that's horrible. My thoughts are running everywhere. I need to focus.

I hope she was dead before they cut her like that, but doubt she was so fortunate. Her face is twisted in a mask of pain and terror and something else I can't place. Is it normal for a body to hold its expression like that after death, or is that unique to our victims? I don't know.

The clarity I felt from my feeding has ebbed completely, replaced by confusion and nausea. Daniel is speaking to a vampire in white coveralls who's examining the knives on the floor, and Trixie is listening eagerly. All I hear is a hum of conversation, not words.

I step closer to the victim. Technically, I'm as dead as she is. It took me a long time to accept that, but it's the truth. What I haven't fully considered before this moment is that there are degrees of death. This one is as dead as they come, and she's not going to come back to tell us who killed her. Not even if we wanted her to. I inhale, just slightly. They say that humans with the blood factor that gives them the potential to become vampires have a strange smell that only we can sense. All I get from this body is dead flesh.

It's a grim scene. Repulsive. But she's better off now, wherever those without the blood factor go when they die. Her suffering is over.

Now it's my turn. I need to help find the ones who did this to her.

I can handle this.

Out of old habit I take a deep breath to calm myself, though death chokes the air.

It's okay. I'm not going to let it affect me.

And then I turn to listen to what an investigator in a black coat is saying about the knives, and I spot three smaller bodies on the floor. Children, drained dry, with their faces frozen in screams.

I race out the back door and vomit into the bushes.

aniel finds me a short while later sitting on one of the saggy-bottomed patio chairs on the back deck, staring up at the stars. I appreciate them so much more than I did when I was alive, now that I can see them clearly. Infinite bright spots against vast, endless darkness. It's a beautiful night. It might even be a perfect one, if I wasn't sitting outside of a human slaughterhouse.

He sits next to me and folds his hands in front of him, resting his forearms on the glass surface of the patio table. He's taken his jacket off, but the cold night doesn't seem to bother him. Mine's gone, too. I shrugged out of it as soon as I finished puking.

"You all right?"

His voice is low. Quiet. Concerned. I should appreciate that, but it makes me feel worse. I'm the only one here who seems to need coddling.

"Yeah. I just needed a minute. Where's Trixie?"

"Taking samples with the techs."

I lean forward and press my palms to my forehead. I feel like my brain is melting. "Of course she is. No problem, right?"

The weight of Daniel's hand rests on my shoulder. I resist the urge to lean into it, and instead focus on the sensation. Daniel's skin is as cold as mine, quite unlike the living touch I felt when my prey grabbed me earlier. He's so damn good at hiding himself. Miranda broadcasts her presence, confident in her position and security, but Daniel is a blank to me.

I relax and take a breath I don't need.

There. Just for a moment, I feel him through his hand. Not his personality—or his spirit, maybe, though we don't have souls—but his power. It's something deeper and darker than what I'd sense in a human. I feel his essence, as though he's let his guard down.

And then it's gone.

"There's nothing wrong with you," he says quietly.

"I think there is." I push my hair off my face and lean back in the chair, and he moves his hand back to the table. "We're not supposed to care about them, are we? We have a responsibility to our stock to keep them safe, and we avoid situations like this because to have this happen regularly would cause panic and expose us to the living world. That's all. We're not supposed to get upset by this."

My voice keeps catching like I'm going to cry. I'm not, though. I've at least come that far.

"Is that what I've taught you?"

"Basically."

He sighs, and I turn to look at him. Daniel doesn't sigh. Daniel doesn't breathe unless he's speaking. He controls his motions and expression unless he needs to pass as living. This little reveal is not so small for him.

I may not be able to feel him most of the time, but I know my trainer.

"Walk with me?" he says. It's not quite the order he would usually deliver, but he's not inviting me to decline. "I think we need to get some air."

I don't point out that there's plenty of air here on the deck, or that technically neither of us needs it. He descends the steps and I follow, shrugging my leather jacket on as we move silently through the shadows to the front of the house.

Daniel leans against the car. Trixie and I jokingly call it the Vampmobile, our trusty steed, but it's Daniel's baby. I won't risk leaning on it and leaving an ass-print in the dust the Trans-Canada has left on its normally shining surface. Instead I shove my hands in my pockets and rock back on my heels, waiting.

He flexes his fingers and crosses his arms. "You're dead, Aviva. You're not a monster. I know I push the idea that you're not human anymore. Maybe too hard, but I have my reasons, especially with you. When I took you from the acclimation facility, the reports on you—"

"Were bad. I know."

His lips narrow. "I was going to say that they indicated specific challenges. Difficulty accepting your new nature. A tendency to cling to your past life, possibly a belief you still had what you thought of as a soul." There's no judgement in his tone, but he glances away as he says *soul*, as though not wishing to embarrass me. "Had I allowed you to think of yourself as even partially human, I would have been encouraging your weaknesses and stifling your potential."

I swallow hard and lower my gaze. "I know. You've helped me so much." I caused problems after my death. Refusing to feed. Believing I was dreaming, that my death had been a nightmare. Cutting myself to watch the wounds heal far too quickly, trying to feel anything that might fill the terrible emptiness left by the absence of my heartbeat.

I made progress at the facility, but I didn't really start accepting my new self until I made friends with Trixie and saw her thriving. Then Daniel plucked us both from those dark rooms and started our hard physical training, and I realized I hadn't lost everything.

When I look up again, he's watching me. Waiting. "We

can't linger in the past," he says. "I suspect you were a kind and compassionate person when you lived. Admirable traits in the living, but they can make the transition difficult. If I'd let you cling to who you were, it would have broken you."

"I know." This is why we're not allowed to stay where we died, why we can't return until everyone we love is dead and everything that might remind us of our life is gone or forgotten.

"I know you know." He narrows his eyes as he studies me. "I've tried to make the separation easier for you by telling you it needs to be complete, that you need to care less about the world of the living. And that is what we aim for. We are not human, and the sooner we understand that, the better it is for us. But it doesn't..." He hesitates, his brow creasing.

I take a step toward him. "What?"

"It doesn't mean you're failing if you don't achieve complete separation from the living right away. It can take some time in a case like yours."

I glance back at the house. "Trixie died not long after me. She's not puking into the bushes right now."

"Trixie wasn't murdered." Daniel's voice is soft, though his eyes never lose their cold edge.

His words hit me like a blow to the chest. I don't know how Trixie died. Or Daniel, or much about who they were in life. It never occurred to me that the people they used to be might still affect them now. I thought it was just me.

He reaches through the open window to take our half-empty coffees from the car, hands me mine, and starts down the street. There's not much risk of us being noticed. No one is interested in being outdoors at this hour on a frigid spring night. A dog tied up outside barks at us, and I shoot it a glance that sends it whimpering into its little chipboard house.

Our kind tend to pass like shadows through the world of the living, as long as we don't draw attention to ourselves. Maybe the living prefer to be ignorant of the predators among them. Sometimes it's easier not to see.

Daniel sips his drink. "Do you remember it at all?"

"Sort of. I try not to think about it. Why, do you want me to talk about it?"

"I think it might help. But that's up to you."

I glance up at him, suspicious. Daniel's not the therapy type. He's more the drop-and-give-me-fifty type. But I suppose things are changing. I'm in the field now, and he's back at his old job. Maybe now that basic training is over, I'll have to adjust to another new reality.

I'd think *God help me* if I wasn't training myself out of that mental habit. There's no help for me there anymore.

I take a cleansing breath and let it out. The visual results are no more impressive than they were on that rooftop across from the church.

"I'd like to tell you," I say slowly, and realize how true this is. Not talking about my past has been a barrier to feeling close to anyone. And though I shouldn't want that, I do. I want to call Daniel a friend.

Daniel nods but looks straight ahead, leaving me room to remember.

"I guess you saw most of it in my file before you took me on," I say. "Born and raised in Ontario, never travelled farther than New Brunswick in my life. Good kid. Didn't get straight A's or anything, but no bother to anyone. Kind of a keener."

He snorts. He wasn't Canadian when he lived, but he's been around long enough to understand.

"My mom died not long after my sister Gracie was born, when I was eight. That was hard, but we survived. And then my dad had a fatal heart attack when I was fourteen. Gracie and I went to live with our grandmother."

My heart still aches to think of it. Gracie never knew our mother, and her Daddy was her world. I'd been through it all once, and having those wounds ripped open again had been unbearable. I'd had a hard time with it. Acted out. Lost friends. Daniel doesn't care about any of that, though, or how I pulled myself out of it when high school ended and I realized I needed to take responsibility for myself and my sister.

"I worked a bit after high school," I tell him. "Grandma didn't have much money or energy, and Gracie... Gracie needed me around. She was having trouble as she got older. Needed guidance."

I blame myself for that even now. I was so lost in my teenage problems, magnified a thousand times by the loss of my parents, that I'd let her drift. Declining loans and university acceptances so I could be around to help her with her homework was too little, too late.

"Gracie was getting into trouble. I always thought of her as a little kid, and I didn't realize how bad things were until it was too late. I'm not sure we ever see other people's struggles as being as big and real as our own, you know?"

Daniel doesn't answer, but he's listening.

"Drugs. Drinking. Sex." I try not to sound too judgmental. At least one of those isn't so different from my own mistakes at a similar age. "Daniel, she was fourteen."

His steps slow. We're rounding the corner at the end of the block. "I often forget how hard it can be to be alive and young," he says. "Unbelievable."

"Not entirely. Things have changed since you were that age. Maybe if I'd believed it sooner, if I hadn't been so caught up in myself, I could have helped her. I tried. I went after her one night. Followed her to a place where her friends were hanging out, this patch of woods behind the mall." I can see it all clearly. "They'd lit a fire, just like their sort did there back when I was in high school."

"Their sort?"

I sigh. "In local terms? Skeets."

He gives me another tight smile. He's heard the word used to describe ignorant, trashy dirtbags. "Enough said."

"The ground was filthy, littered with bottles and garbage. Couple of dirty sleeping bags." That had come as no surprise. I'd scouted the area earlier that week, during daylight hours. "All these kids were standing around and drinking, wearing matching black jackets like they were a fucking gang or something when they were just a bunch of suburban brats with issues. I didn't even consider the idea that they might be carrying weapons."

I can't help the dread that crawls over my skin. It's like I'm watching everything on a screen now, wanting to scream out to the characters before me to stop, but they won't. Everything is done. This is just the replay.

"I was just going to confront Gracie at home after I confirmed what she was up to. Get her help, somehow. But as I watched them, this kid slapped her. Backhanded her right across the face. He was big, too, and older than her." In my mind I see Gracie—my little sister, my pain in the ass, my everything even when she was acting like a punk— fall to the ground. And that bastard strutting like a peacock. That was what set me off. His fucking pride in putting her in her place. I remember how my blood raced as my heart pounded. My last great adrenaline rush.

"I yelled, and they all stopped and stared at me. I tried to help Gracie up, but she pulled away from me. She was hurt, but it was like this was no big deal. Like me embarrassing her was worse than getting hit. I didn't know what to do. I was angry. At her as much as him by that point, but she was already on the ground, so I turned on him. I wasn't thinking. Just screaming, hitting him back, asking how he liked it. I might as well have been smacking a boulder for all it hurt him."

I won't admit as much to Daniel, but I'd love to get my hands on him now that I could do some real damage.

"Gracie yelled for me to stop, to go home, to let it go and wait up for her and we'd talk later. She still sounded embarrassed, but there was real fear there. The rest of them were laughing. A couple of the guys joked about it, this big guy getting beat up by a tiny girl. He pulled a gun out of his pocket, and I backed away. That shut most of them up, but a few kept on. Called him a pussy. One said, 'Pull the trigger, asshole!'"

Like a joke. I remember that clearly.

"And he did. Aimed it sideways like a perfect asshole, took a step back. Stumbled over a root. Pulled the trigger."

Daniel raises his thick eyebrows. "An imitation gangster shot you because you yelled at him?"

"I don't think he knew it was loaded. Or maybe the shot was an accident." I remember the shock on the kid's face as the gun recoiled and I staggered backward. Gracie's screams, louder than anyone else's shouts. The smell of melting rubber as I stumbled backward through the fire.

My killer dropping the gun like it was a snake about to bite him and taking off into the forest.

None of it is supposed to matter now, but it's seared into my mind. "He didn't mean to kill me."

"But he did."

"Yeah, he did. Shot me somewhere below my heart." I'm not totally sure where. The wound was healed when I woke up as a vampire. "I doubt he could have aimed that well if he was sober. Bad luck for both of us." I pause. "Anyway, I guess I got off lucky compared with our adult victim in there. My death was quick, if not painless."

"Someone who loved you saw it, though."

"Yeah." I get what he means about why this crime scene would affect me. Tears are gathering in my eyes for the first time in ages. Incredible. They're not warm, but they're real. "Gracie just kept screaming, and someone yelled at her to shut up. They all ran, except Gracie and this other kid who rolled up his coat and made it into a pillow for me. He went to call for help, but I think he knew it was too late."

I don't remember the blood. I didn't have the strength to look down to assess the damage. I remember how heavy my body felt, though, the pressure in my chest and the white fog that crowded my mind.

"I wanted to say something to Gracie, to tell her I loved her and I was sorry, but there wasn't time. It was so damned fast, though I feel like I held on for longer than I should have been able to."

Daniel nods. "That's not unusual for someone with the blood factor. For people born with the potential for existence after death, we seem to cling rather hard to life."

His voice has taken on the vaguest hint of an accent. Something British, maybe, but I've never been good with placing it. He only lets it slip like that when he's reminiscing, so I don't get to hear it much. It's nice.

"Do you remember your heart stopping?" he asks.

"Yeah. And even after that. The police and ambulance coming. Someone saying I was dead, but I was still there. But at the same time, I kind of knew they were right."

Daniel smiles slightly, as if at some long-buried memory.

"I drifted off then. This peaceful black cloud came over me, and I felt like things would be okay. And the next thing I remember is waking up strapped to a hospital bed, screaming." I don't know what happened to Gracie, or to the kid who killed me. I don't know where they are now. I probably could find out, but I really do understand why we have these rules. I could so easily become obsessed with a life that's not mine anymore, and I don't want that.

Aviva Siobhan Walker died that night. I'm just Aviva now. I want so badly to move forward and find out exactly what that means, but it's been hard to let go.

"And you had your difficult transition period after

that," Daniel adds. He pauses before speaking again. "Do you hate them? Whoever turned you?"

I have to think about that for a second. "Sometimes. There are times when I'm glad to be what I am. Usually when I'm feeding. Sometimes when we're training, when I'm using strength I didn't have when I was alive." I look up at the sky again. "When I realize how much bigger the world is than I ever understood before, when I feel like I might be getting a tiny inkling of where I fit into it all. But those are the high points. When things are low, or quiet, or when I'm hungry and have time to really think about what I am and how my existence depends on stealing life from others, when I—"

I can't let myself finish the thought that comes to mind —one that starts with people filing into a church and ends with the phrase, *She's with God now*. I know how untrue that sentiment is and always will be in my case. It's too much, and Daniel has to be at the limit of his sympathy by now.

"Times like those, yeah. I hate whoever made me. Whoever recognized what I was, stuck around until I was dead, and then didn't let me slip away."

He nods slowly. "I understand that completely. It does get easier, though."

I want to ask what he means. How he died. But we're almost back at the house.

"I can't say I'm sorry you became what you are,

though," he tells me, one corner of his mouth lifting in a smile. "You're a pain in my ass. You have problems. But I still see in you what I saw when I took you from the facility. You have potential. And quite frankly, I think Trixie would have me driven mad by now if I only had her around."

I laugh, as much out of surprise as actually seeing the humour in his words. "Careful, Daniel. I might get the idea you like me."

He glares sideways. "Not in the least."

I smile. That's more like it. But this has been good. I feel lighter now than I did before. Stronger for sharing my sad little story. And maybe a little closer to letting it go.

We turn up the driveway, and Daniel pauses near the hood of the car. "Might I ask you for an unrelated favour?"

"Sure." He never has before. Daniel does not ask. Daniel demands. This is the foundation of our relationship.

"Keep an eye on Trixie if I get called away."

I'm not sure what to say. If anything, I'd expect him to ask Trixie to watch me. "Why?"

He looks up at the front window of the house. Though the blackout curtains are closed, I see hints of movement. The other half of the duplex is dark and empty. "It's nothing. Forget I said anything." He shakes his head. "Caring too little can be as dangerous as caring too much, even if it doesn't leave you puking in the bushes."

"Daniel?"

But he's gone, hurrying toward the back door. I guess our discussion is over, and it's up to me to decide what I want to do now. He hasn't ordered me back in, but I force my heavy feet to carry me after him.

This is what I am now, and I have a job to do.

CHAPTER SEVEN

The kitchen is just as we left it, if a bit colder thanks to our comings and goings. Someone has turned off the electric baseboard heaters. The bodies are where they lay when I fled. Woman on the table, children dumped in a heap on the floor like discarded beer cans. I force myself to look at them. The oldest might be eight years old, a girl with curly brown hair and terrified blue eyes, dressed in a blue princess nightgown. The next, a towheaded boy with a crazy cowlick at the front of his hair, might have been old enough to start school, but I doubt it.

And then the baby. Not a year old, probably. I'm a bad judge. Never cared for babies. His chubby legs are folded under him, back arched, mouth frozen in a scream.

I didn't do this. But I can't help remembering how hard it was for me to stop feeding earlier when my victim was so fresh and unused. His strength still flows through me. He was there by choice, and I let him leave alive, but I'm not as different from whoever killed these children as I'd like to imagine.

I had no choice in becoming what I am. I wish it didn't frighten me at times like this, when I consider what I could so easily become.

No. I am stronger than these rogues. I will never take a life, no matter how tempting it may be. Rogues are criminals, justifiably cast out from society, hunted for their crimes and executed. And execution for a vampire means oblivion. No heaven. No afterlife. This is it.

I make a silent promise to the children that I'll do whatever I can to see their killers put to true death in what I hope will be the most painful way possible. It doesn't make me feel better, but it's something. It's a purpose. A defense against what I could easily become if I lost control.

A dark shape flickers at the edge of my vision, but when I turn, there's nothing there.

Daniel and Trixie are already in the living room, chatting with the technician and the investigator, waiting for the clean-up crew. Some day I'll learn the ins and outs of how we cover up a mess like this, dealing with human police, nosy neighbours, reporters who might come sniffing around like bloodhounds hot on the trail. For now, I'm just thankful it's not my responsibility. I can't imagine it will be easy with this one. Rogues are supposed to be secretive.

Furtive. I thought they'd cover their tracks, not wanting to be hunted down.

This is... this is fucking *brazen*.

Trixie gives me a concerned look, which I wave off. I'm thinking maybe no one else saw me flee until the technician shoots me a strange look from beneath her long lashes and smirks.

I've never heard a vampire gossip, but I'm sure word will get around somehow. Fantastic.

Daniel watches me from his position beside the sofa. He's the only one not sitting. There's no trace of the sympathetic almost-friend of a few minutes ago. He's all business now, listening carefully, nodding as the investigator says there's nothing more to see.

Daniel turns to Trixie. "What do you think?"

She shrugs. "Blood samples from the kitchen match the mother, at least in type. It makes sense. She wasn't the one they fed from." She sounds like she's been doing this forever. Just another body. No sweat. "It's too late for us to get any blood evidence of what the younger victims were experiencing when they died—they're totally dry—but I think it's easy to see they were terrified." She turns to the technician. "Right?"

"You got it."

Everyone looks at me, waiting for my thoughts. I want to slink back into the kitchen, but I won't. The technician smirks again, looking like she's about to say something. Trixie frowns. Daniel's not giving me anything.

I'm not going to look foolish again.

"It was vampires, no question," I begin, remembering the wounds on the children and the bite marks on the mother. "The youngest was bled from the femoral artery rather than the neck, but it's all consistent. Rogues, obviously. This isn't a sanctioned feeding zone, the mother isn't one of ours, and none of the others were old enough to be legal stock." Obvious stuff that anyone here could see for themselves. Not good enough if I want to impress them.

"What else?" Daniel asks. His gaze has grown sharp, and it's making me uncomfortable. But he's right. I already know more than this surface shit.

My mouth goes dry. "They wanted the fear." This part makes me uncomfortable. I glance at Trixie, but if she's making any connection in her mind between these victims and her own dark tastes earlier this evening, it's not troubling her. I relax slightly. Whatever our inclinations, there are lines most of us won't cross. "Rather than coming to the club and inducing it in a willing human, they tied this woman up and tortured her while her children watched, then fed from them when their terror was at its peak. Which I would guess means these aren't garden-variety rogues." I shake my head and try not to let my disgust overwhelm me. "They're not feeding because they have to, but because they want to."

My voice grows calm, my thoughts clear and analytical. I think harder about the scene, about my walk with Daniel. "The other half of this house is unoccupied. There are no curtains in the windows over there, and the snow drifts in the driveway don't look like they've been shovelled in a while. Whoever did this has been watching this family, or might have found them through real estate ads. They didn't want anyone to hear the screaming."

"They planned well," says the investigator in a mild Irish accent. He's removed his black coat, revealing a sharply tailored pinstripe suit. Black shirt, black tie, almost-black hair slicked back. He could be a banker. Or a gangster.

"It also seems like they didn't much care whether anyone stumbled on their mess," I add. It's all I've got, but I suppose it's enough. Daniel relaxes.

"That is unusual," the investigator says, "but not unheard of." He goes to the window and runs his index finger over the sealant.

"Note this, as well," he says, and motions for me and Trixie to come closer. "New windows, energy-efficient. Excellent sound insulation. All replaced recently. Whoever did this chose ideal killing grounds." He holds out a hand, and I shake it. "Wallace. I don't believe we had the pleasure earlier."

"Aviva," I say, nearly stuttering. I don't often introduce

myself to other vampires, and it feels strange to not have a last name to append to it anymore.

Wallace looks deep into my eyes and gives me a wink so quick I almost miss it, then turns to Daniel. "They're doing well. Will they be following you through this assignment?"

"No." Daniel's voice is firm. "Investigation only. No hunting. They're not ready."

"We are!" Trixie protests. Daniel shoots her a look that shuts her up before she can get another word out. He won't tolerate us making him look bad.

He did warn us about that.

My thoughts drift back to the kitchen. I can't help thinking I've missed something. Not the windows, though I should have remembered that detail. This is something ephemeral. A feeling, not a physical detail I should have noted.

I wander away from the conversation, back toward the bodies. No one mentioned fingerprints, so I assume there weren't any, or that it doesn't matter. If there was anything here that would tell us who did this, Wallace and Daniel would be all over it.

I think over what little I know about rogues from the few times Daniel talked about his hunting days. They don't stay in any one city for long. Our elders keep each other informed of their presence if they cause trouble, at which time the hunters deal with the problem swiftly and without mercy, often crossing clan territory lines with the elders' permission. I can see why Daniel's stories would make Trixie eager to join the hunt. It's a hard job, but Daniel spoke of it fondly—usually while contrasting it with the hardship of his current assignment.

But it's not just an exciting opportunity to see the world and catch bad guys. Seeing this kitchen makes me understand how serious the hunts really are. The rogues that attacked here aren't just an inconvenience for us, or even the ultimate horror for this family. If word of this got out, if the living knew we existed outside of their stories and their nightmares, if they had even the slightest under-standing of the unquenchable blood lust that comes over even the most civilized among us when we haven't fed for too long... No. The situation would be unthinkable.

This is why we have things set up the way we do. We know what happens when the living feel that they must kill or be killed.

It seems disrespectful to leave the woman naked and exposed on the table. I glance up at the dark staircase heading to the upper level from the kitchen. There's a basket of folded laundry there, and I take one of the quilts from it and cover the children first. Something catches in my chest as their frightened eyes disappear, as they lose sight of their mother.

They can't see, I remind myself. They're gone. They're safe.

Fear suddenly courses through me, high and fluttering in my throat. I close my eyes. Behind my eyelids, shadows move around the room, quick and graceful and terrifying. An echo of high-pitched laughter rings through my mind, and a deafening scream follows. It's all gone when I open my eyes, but the feeling is worse. I'm afraid like I haven't been since I left the facility. Afraid like these people were. It's not enough to set my heart pounding, but even without physical response, the feeling is unmistakable.

I'm losing my mind. Hallucinating. I must be.

After a minute of standing perfectly still, the feeling ebbs, leaving anxiety where there was terror. I can handle this, unpleasant though it may be.

I blink hard to clear my head and grab another blanket to place over the naked form on the table. I close her eyes, careful to only touch her with the blanket, not my bare hands. I'm not wearing gloves.

That's better. I should have done that with the others. It makes her look more peaceful.

"What happened?" I whisper as I cover her.

"She's not going to answer you." Trixie is leaning in the doorway, watching me. Concerned.

"I know." I motion her closer. "Trix, have you ever seen a body that could be... you know. Like us?"

She shakes her head, setting her hair bouncing. "I'm not sure I'd know one if I saw it, though I'm told I would. Daniel's never really told me the difference. Smell, or something? Even if I did, though, I couldn't, like..." Her already pallid skin lightens a shade. "No thanks."

I couldn't either, I'm sure. When I was alive, I thought vampires were made when a living person was bitten. I mean, I didn't think they were made outside of stories, but I thought that was how the theory went. The truth is that it's not so simple, and definitely not pleasant. It starts with a body. A corpse, but not just any corpse—one with the blood factor that makes our transformation possible. In most cases a clan will have identified this person and watched them for a time, assessing them, seeing whether they'll make the transition easily or whether their corpse should be left to rot. I suppose they look for the traits that make Trixie so good at what she is. Cunning, cleverness, resilience, strength, and a healthy dose of self-interest. Everything I'm not.

An exasperated nurse at the facility once let it slip that I wasn't chosen. No one approved my change. No one was informed until it was done. For all I know, a rogue with a grudge against civilized vampires did it and dumped me so some clan would have to care for me through my terrible adjustment.

I doubt anyone would be that committed to a practical joke, though. The transformation process is horrible for the maker. Within a few hours after death, the vampire has to drain the dead blood by mouth, consuming every drop of it.

It's unbearable to think of. Living blood brings us

something close to life, but dead blood depletes us. I'm told that the taste is vile, that it becomes thick and dark, that the one consuming it can easily succumb to the despair and pain it brings. To go through all that, to create a new vampire, is considered a great sacrifice.

And not one that's always appreciated by the recipient.

"Would you do it?" Trixie asks.

"What, right now?"

"Yeah. Like, if you knew you could drain her or one of those kids, give them what we have, would you?"

"Absolutely not. Do you think they'd want to come back after what they've gone through?" Never mind how terrible it would be for the children. Their brains wouldn't develop any more. They'd never mature, not in a hundred years.

"Just asking. I don't think I could." She sticks her finger down her throat and mimes gagging. I try not to take the gesture personally. If she heard me retching earlier, she wouldn't make fun of me for it.

I hope.

I don't want to look around anymore, but this is why we're here, and I'm not keen to go back to the living room with that technician and her knowing glances. Much as I might want to switch to another career in the future, this is my assignment tonight.

Whoever did this cleaned it up well. Not the blood and

human mess, but the traces the attackers might have left. The woman on the table is filthy, but the fingernails visible beneath the edge of the blanket have been scrubbed clean. Parts of the floor have been wiped down, leaving no footprints. The technicians will have measured the bite marks, but until we have suspects to compare them to, they're useless.

Trixie watches me for a few minutes as I look on top of the fridge, inside the cupboards, behind the microwave. I give the flesh in the glass bowl a once-over. It's less horrible without the victim watching.

Wallace, Daniel, and the technician enter the room. "Second time this month," Wallace says as he watches me poking around. He nods at the bowl. "Though this little detail is new."

"When did they all die?" I ask.

"These ones, early this morning. Very early, after a night of... well." He nods at the blanket covering the body on the table, gives me an odd look, but doesn't ask about what I've done. "The one before that was the middle of the afternoon. They're getting bold, taking chances with times and locations." His gaze flashes to the children's bodies huddled under their quilt, just for a moment. "With their victims."

Daniel flexes his fingers, popping the knuckles. I keep thinking he's broken the habit, and then there it is again. I guess it's hard to break one after so many years. "We'll just hope they become bold enough to make a mistake next time."

"Next time?" I didn't know I was going to speak until it happens. Everyone looks at me. I fight to sound like I'm interested rather than horrified. "You don't think we'll find them before they kill again?"

"Nothing here to go on," Wallace says as he shrugs into his trenchcoat. "I doubt they're ready to move on, though, so we'll have our chance soon enough."

The silence grows awkward. Trixie rolls her shoulders back in a deep stretch. "Well, then. Pleasant as it is here, I'm about ready to go home if we're all done."

The technician nods at the blankets before she steps out the door. "I suppose these folks will be cozy enough until the crew comes to move them."

I don't react to her tone. She's right. I shouldn't have covered them if I didn't want anyone thinking I was weird. It's probably too late for that, anyway, but I could have made more of an effort.

"So we're just leaving them?" I meant for it to sound like a casual question, but there's a note of desperation in my voice that contrasts starkly with my cold analysis in the living room. Trixie shifts her weight onto one leg, hands on hips, giving me what she probably means to be a sympathetic glance.

Wallace pauses on his way to the door and turns back to give Daniel a questioning look as a door slams outside. The cleaners are here to make the victims disappear.

My throat tightens.

Daniel steps close enough that he looms over me. "There's nothing you can do for them now," he says quietly. Not pleading with his voice, but there's something in his eyes that's begging me to shut up. This could be far more embarrassing for him than Trixie's excessive enthusiasm.

"We're going to let it happen again." I don't ask. I accuse, if quietly. It seems I wasn't so far off in my assessment of our attitudes toward the living, and I wonder how much of Daniel's sympathy toward my emotions earlier was just to perk me up and get me back into the house to save face.

Daniel looks back at Wallace, who is definitely not leaving until he sees how this plays out.

Daniel's expression hardens completely as he turns back to me. "We're keeping our stock safe. Our job is to cover this up until it happens again, and then we get more information. Or we deal with it until these rogues get uncomfortable with our investigation, move on, and become someone else's problem. Wouldn't be the first time." He lifts the blanket up from the table, glances beneath, and steps away. "Taking care of bodies isn't my job. Be glad it's not yours."

There's a *yet* there. I hear it in his voice, a subtle

reminder that I'm not on a good path right now, that it's only thanks to his patience that I'm not out on my ass, joining the clean-up crew.

I bite back defensive anger that wants to make me lash out at him. There's no point, and embarrassing him further will only make things worse for me.

I swallow hard, fighting back the anger that's replaced the fear that nearly overcame me earlier. It hasn't hit me this hard in a while, this disgust with how we talk about the living, as though they're nothing to us. Daniel's not usually this blunt about it, but he's never voiced a contrary opinion, either. Trixie has no problem with it. Neither does anyone else, judging by the relieved look Wallace gives Daniel as he exits the house.

Daniel looks like he has more to say, but he turns to leave.

I follow him and Trixie to the car, ignoring the dark van and the vampires in grey uniforms heading for the back door of the house. I have no choice but to leave. But I let Trixie take shotgun this time.

I don't feel like talking.

I close my eyes as Daniel starts the engine. The terrifying shadows are gone. I remember the laughter, but that's all it is. A memory, not a hallucination. Maybe I'm not going crazy, after all.

Maybe.

CHAPTER EIGHT

ome is a townhouse near the old beating heart of St. John's. It's not as conspicuous as the Jellybean Row houses that show up on postcards and tourism websites, but the look is similar: turquoise siding, white window frames, and a door that Trixie insists on repainting every time the mood strikes her. This month it's violet. Last time it was bright rose, which replaced a pea-soup green. By next week it could be yellow.

I certainly don't mind. It's a remnant of the free spirit I suspect she was in life, sort of like the ever-changing hues of her hair. It's nice to know we all hold on to something. Trixie's fortunate that her remnants of her old self all seem relatively shallow, and therefore tolerable in a new vampire.

The inside of the house suits us all just fine. Living

room and eat-in kitchen down below, Trixie's and my bedrooms a flight up, and Daniel's territory on the third level. He stays out of our space except to pass through or use the shower, and we're not invited up to his. Daniel might seem almost friendly when we're not actively training and Trixie's not actively pissing him off, but separation suits his role as our elder and our trainer.

Distance. Respect. Rules.

Only occasionally does he have to thump on the floor to get us to shut up when he's trying to get to sleep.

Tonight, Trixie and I speak in whispers as we chat in her room, dressed in pyjamas—adorable nightie for her, long pants and a white camisole for me—with a pot of hot tea on the bed between us. Daniel is upstairs already. He shut down completely on the short drive home, scowling out the windshield, refusing to speak. Trixie tried a few times to start a conversation about how she and I might help with the rogues, but Daniel wouldn't have it. He left us as soon as he walked through the door, checking a message on his old flip phone as he climbed the stairs.

He's not obligated to explain himself to us, but this isn't like him. While he'd be well within his rights to take a "because I said so" approach with us, he tends to only demand unquestioning obedience when we're in physical training. Otherwise, he lets us ask, even if he doesn't always answer. The fact that he allows this, while apparently obeying his own orders from his superiors without question, is just one more of his little mysteries.

"I don't know what crawled up his ass," Trixie says, squeezing a lemon wedge and watching the juice roll over her fingers and into her tea. "He was fine until we left that house. Maybe he didn't get a good feed in earlier."

I flop back on the white bedspread. "Maybe he's sick of my issues."

"Probably. You've got to let it go, Viva. You're going to get a reputation." She wrinkles her nose. "And not the good kind. What happened tonight, anyway?"

There was a time when my back would have gone up at her talking down to me, heaping on advice like a superior big sister, but it's just her way. She means well, and talking things out helps. "I don't know. I just... didn't it bother you at all, walking in there and seeing those bodies?"

"No."

"Even the children?"

She sighs. "It was sad, yeah. But it wasn't my fault. I didn't know them, I didn't kill them. And they weren't our stock."

"No, I know. It was just a shock, maybe because—" I pause. For some reason I don't feel like explaining about my death. I'm not even convinced that's the reason I freaked out. Maybe that was just Daniel trying to justify my failure. "I don't know. It's hard to not care. I reacted, and I shouldn't have."

Trixie sips her tea and stretches out beside me, lying on her side. "And after, when you went back in and covered them? You looked like you were going to have a panic attack or something."

My stomach knots again at the memory. "I don't know. Just a blip."

"A blip?"

"Yeah. Something screwy in my mind. A momentary perception issue. It passed."

I won't tell her about the screams, the shadows. Nor will I tell Daniel. I don't need this in my file.

She frowns and sits up. "It sucks for them that they died. But it's not our job to protect the living. We're not superheroes or angels or anything."

Sometimes I feel like Trixie and I are perfectly matched as friends. At other times, I wonder whether I understand her at all. "Doesn't your conscience bother you, though, when you realize that our existence as a species led to this?"

"Conscience?"

I roll my eyes. "Yeah. Conscience. The little voice that sits on your shoulder and whispers in your ear that a thing is wrong."

She sips her tea delicately, pinky outstretched. "Oh, that," she says. "No, I caught that little motherfucker years ago and crushed him under my boot. Improved my life immensely, let me tell you."

I stare at the ceiling, unsure of what to say to that. She's probably not wrong. If we vampires have morals, they're to serve ourselves and our clans, not the greater good of the world. "But we need the living," I say, trying another angle. I need her to understand so I'll feel less like a complete failure here.

She gives her head a firm shake. "We need our stock. The feeders. That's it. Even then, one's pretty much like any other. Not a big loss if we lose one. We just keep them safe because that makes them trust us and saves us a shit-load of trouble."

"I know." I've heard it enough times that I'm going to scream if someone says it again. We are not human. We are vampire. We are the hunters, they are the prey. We just don't let them see it.

"Try looking at it this way," Trixie says, setting down her cup on the nightstand. "I mean, I was weirded out at first, too. You care about them because you feel a connection to them."

"I *was* them, Trixie. So were you, just a few years ago. You were alive as a human far longer than you've been a vampire."

She presses her lips together as though mustering her patience. "Yes. But—and pay attention, now, because I'm about to drop a whole lot of wisdom on your pretty little head."

I roll onto my side and rest my head on one hand. "I'm all ears."

Trixie leans closer. "Even when we were alive, we were special. We had the blood factor that prepared us for this. We just didn't know it. We're not like them. You care about the living as though you're looking after your family, when in fact they are no more like us than... than a cave man would be to them."

"Fine. But we were raised by those cave men."

She throws her hands up, melodramatic to her core. "You're hopeless. Completely hopeless."

I drink my tea burning hot, just like Trixie does. It's fun to feel warm inside, and I need something pleasant now that the good feelings from my feeding have left me. When things are quiet we can go for almost a week without food. I'm wondering now how much more often we'll have to feed when we're doing this kind of stressful, draining work. Three times a week? Daily? I could go for a bite now if I could afford it, but we'll have to wait until Daniel takes us back to the Inferno.

My thoughts circle back to my meal. To my overwhelming hunger before I fed and the temptations my prey brought with him. No, we're not like the living. I am not the creature I was the night I died, or any day before that.

Maybe Trixie is right. What if I let go and accepted that I'm not like them? If instead of berating myself for wanting to finish off my prey tonight, I revelled in my power and my choice to let him live? I can see how much easier that would be. How much less tempting it would be to fuck up and do things like covering dead bodies as though they deserved that dignity.

The thought could fit. For the first time, I understand that I could slip into it like a pair of jeans that just needs a little breaking in to feel perfectly comfortable.

And yet, I can't. Not yet. I can't help feeling like I'd lose myself if I let that idea overtake me.

I sigh and drain my tea cup. I'll keep Trixie's words in mind, anyway, for the next time the shadows threaten and I'm in danger of making a fool of myself.

What a mess I am.

"The thing is, Trixie, I can't—"

"Shh, he's coming."

I open myself to him, but Daniel might as well be a ghost for all I can feel him right now. It's only the creak of the second stair up from our floor that announces him to me. I expect him to continue down, but he stops to look into the room. Trixie shrieks and pretends to swoon as I struggle to sit up.

"Daniel, we're in our unmentionables!" she cries in a feathery, high-pitched voice, and rests an arm dramatically over her eyes. Her short nightie is slightly less mentionable than my own attire, but it doesn't matter either way. Daniel's never interested in ogling.

"I'm going out," he says. "And for the record, there's nothing up my ass, my feeding was fine, and I'm not upset with you, Aviva. I just need a break. Understood?"

Trixie sits up. "Can we at least discuss the possibility of—"

"No. I'll be back around dawn. Try not to wake the neighbours."

Trixie glares at the empty doorframe after he's gone and the front door slams closed behind him. "He treats us like children. We could do so much more than just poking around the rogues' leftovers." She chews her bottom lip. "Can you imagine how thrilling it would be to track, to hunt, to chase? It's in our nature, Viva. Maybe if you were allowed to let that out, you'd really feel what you are. Get that separation from the living."

"Maybe. Listen, I'm going to bed."

She waves me off and reaches for the blue nail polish on her bedside table.

It's not her attitude toward them that's bothering me, or her insane desire to put herself in danger, which I sort of envy. Much as I resist it, there's a part of me that longs for the level of acceptance that came so easily for her.

I actually don't know why I want to be alone right now. Maybe I've just got too much going on in my head for me to want more conversation rattling around in there.

There's a note on my bed. I don't even know when Daniel stopped to leave it.

Aviva—
We need to talk privately. Later.
Daniel

Short and sweet, the perfect opposite of Daniel himself. My stomach twists slowly into a knot as I ponder what this might mean. Maybe he saw my almost-freak-out with the shadows. Maybe he *is* mad at me for embarrassing him in front of Wallace, but has enough class to not demote me in front of Trixie.

I drop the note on my dresser and put on some loud music, neighbours be damned.

I've got thoughts that need drowning.

CHAPTER NINE

The city is breathtaking from the top of Cabot Tower, a black-velvet expanse of harbour drawn up tight against the glittering landscape that is downtown, with the rest of the city glowing behind it. The weather's not always clear here, as the tourism commercials imply. But that's why we stay—for days when daylight is less of a danger, as long as we're careful.

And then there are the nights, of course. There's nothing like a clear night, when we can get out and—

A hard slap to the back of my head knocks my thoughts off track.

"Ow!" I shout, and Daniel swats me again. "Quit it! I'm still preparing." I'm supposed to be finding my focus, locating the deeper part of myself that should be able to sense him coming. I've found it before. It helps if I've fed, as I did tonight before we came out here. I'm just not there yet.

"You don't get time-outs in a fight to prepare yourself. You're lucky I'm going easy on you."

His hand whips through the air toward my face. I clear my mind as he's taught me, and my own hand flies up without conscious direction and blocks him. Muscle memory, the payoff for months upon months of getting my ass kicked by this monster. I deflect his other hand as it cuts through the air toward me, but his boot in my side takes me by surprise and sends me flying off the tower onto the cannon platform fifteen metres below. I land flat on my back with a graceless thud and gasp at the pain that shoots through every part of my body.

This won't finish me. Not even close. But my muscles burn where he kicked me, and my back stiffens in spasms. I've learned to disregard pain. That doesn't mean I don't feel it.

Guess he's done going easy on me.

"Get up," he orders from the top of the tower. "Come after me."

My mouth twists into a snarl, and I force myself to my feet. I asked for this. He came home and slept all day, then said nothing to me about his note. I suggested a private training session in light of my recent problems, and he agreed.

I'd sort of hoped for a little more conversation and a

little less hurtling toward the ground at sixty kilometres per hour, but I'll take this as a sign that he's not firing me yet.

It occurs to me that I would miss this if he reassigned me. I would miss the challenge, and even the aches I get in my body after I learn from a half dozen mistakes. I'd miss Daniel.

Holy shit. This is almost getting to be fun.

No matter. He's pissed me off, now, and I'm not about to get all weepy about what could happen in the future.

"I thought you wanted to talk," I say, hoping I can get his exact location from his answer.

"I do. Hurry up." We don't have to yell to be heard, which is good. We were alone up here when we arrived, but a couple of kids have just arrived in the parking lot to look at the city lights.

Or whatever they're doing.

Daniel has moved down to the lookout balcony, and I decide to approach from above. It takes me some time to scale the rough stone wall, and I hesitate before I reach the top. It will be impossible for me to sneak up on him, no matter what my approach.

"They parked right beside you," I say quietly, ignoring the shake in my arms as I grip the lip of rock at the top of the tower. I'm not worried about my voice giving me away. He can feel me already. "Shit, if he opens his door and the wind catches it…"

I clear my mind again and focus on Daniel as I pull

myself up and creep over the upper roof of the tower. He's left himself open. I should probably be insulted, but I'm glad I can practice tracking my quarry. "Idiots," he mutters, and a small change in my perception of him confirms the shift in his attention.

He won't give me more than a few seconds, and I doubt that he's really distracted, but it's all I'm going to get. I launch myself at him, and he sidesteps my attack, leaving me to land cat-like on my toes. There's no time for me to congratulate myself for that. I dodge a fist aimed at my nose and attempt to speed up my perceptions. It's one of Trixie's gifts, not mine, but she's taught me a few tricks. It requires a lot of energy to maintain that level of perception, though, and even then I can't keep it up for more than a second or two. It's a good thing we fed tonight.

I duck under another swing and head-butt Daniel in the stomach, sending him staggering a few steps back. It doesn't have the effect it would on someone living, since Daniel can't have the wind knocked out of him, but it's one more thing for him to react to.

He grabs the back of my jacket before I can right myself and hauls me up, ready to toss me over the edge again. I twist myself around as he lifts me and wrap my legs around his waist, locking tight to him, clamping my arms around his head so that my body blocks his vision.

He stops moving, lets go, and holds his hands out to the

side. "What the fuck, Aviva?" His voice is muffled by the front of my shirt.

I don't trust him. If I let go, my ass is going to end up on the pavement.

"Get off," he mumbles.

"Can't."

"This is asinine."

At least, I think that's what he's saying. Hard to tell.

"It worked, though," I point out. "Say I won."

He pulls his head back and glares up at me. "Fine. But only because I don't have a weapon and I'm feeling too kindly toward you to attempt ramming you into that brick wall."

"Whatever. I stopped you."

He growls, exposing his fangs. "Get your boobs out of my face before I bite them off."

Oh. I hesitate a moment too long as I realize that this may not be entirely professional of me. I land lightly on my toes and hop up to sit on the low balcony wall, swinging my legs over the edge so I can face the city lights. Daniel sits beside me and shakes his head.

"That was the worst ending to a fight I've ever experienced."

"It's not Hollywood, Daniel. Whatever works."

We sit shoulder to shoulder, ignoring whatever those kids in the car below are up to. They won't pay any attention to us. Daniel has a knack for making himself unnoticeable that goes far beyond most vampires. One of his particular gifts, I suppose.

I can't help being aware of the spot where our arms touch. It's by no means a first. Physical contact is a daily reality, and we've been sharing a shower and a coffeemaker for a year.

But things are changing. Our roles are changing. And he seems... different.

Or maybe that's because I can't stop thinking about him nibbling my tits, now that he's mentioned it. Asshole.

"What did you want to talk to me about?"

He reaches for the orange paper cup he left sitting on the ledge when we got here and takes a sip. "How are you doing, Aviva?"

Oh, fantastic. We're in empathy mode again. "I'm fine. Really. Last night was a bit overwhelming at first, but I can handle it. Trixie gave me some good ideas I'm thinking over, and I'm sure I can distance myself next time."

Now that we're getting down to it, I realize I definitely don't want to get kicked off the crew. A chill that has nothing to do with the cold wind creeps over my skin. Maybe he's being nice to soften the blow.

"I know you can distance yourself. But do you want to?"

It's a trick question, obviously. He made his opinions on my doubts abundantly clear at the crime scene last night, and no matter how understanding he may be of my personal situation, I know he needs me to suck it up and act like a proper vampire. *Yes* is the right answer, but if I say it, he'll know I'm lying.

"Not especially," I confess, knowing this might seal his decision to find me a new place. Like rehoming a puppy that's cute, but won't stop shitting on the sofa. "I know what you're going to say, and I think you should reconsider. Even if you're right."

He continues to watch the city, not so much as glancing at me. "You think you know me so well?"

His voice has slipped out of its plain-as-cardboard North American accent again. Either he's taking his mask off, or he wants me to think he is.

"I've known you for more than a year, Daniel. I've lived with you. Trained under you. Learned from you. I know you."

He arches one eyebrow and finally turns to me. "You know what I've let you know. I have my secrets, Miss Viva." He reaches up to rub the back of his neck. "But yes, you know what I'm supposed to say now. That you're not suited for this work, not if you can't understand the true place of the living in our world."

My stomach cramps up.

"But I've been thinking about our talk last night," he says, "and about what happened after. It's not just a lingering attachment to your humanity, is it? You really care about them."

I feel like I should apologize for that, but I can't. "I try not to."

"I know. And I can't help wondering if maybe that's where we've gone wrong in your training."

I shift away so I can turn toward him for a better look. No, it's still Daniel sitting there. Embrace-your-vampire-nature, never-admit-a-mistake Daniel. "Excuse me?"

He looks away again, frowning. "I see you struggling with trying to suppress your humanity. You have days when you seem to be letting it go, but those are the days when we're not around them. I saw you watching those people going into that church, acting like you were just killing time, but you were remembering, weren't you?"

I just nod. He's obviously thought this speech through, and I don't want to interrupt. This level of openness is unprecedented for him, at least with me.

"I'd guess you were thinking about how they could go in there," he continues, "and how you can't. How you're not one of them anymore. Not a creature of breath and light."

There's no point even agreeing. He obviously knows me far better than I know him.

"So I worry about that." His frown deepens, carving lines between his eyes and tightening his jaw. "Not so much about how you hang on to it, but about what a struggle it's become for you. I know you want to do well in your training, even if you haven't exactly figured out where you want it to take you. But you seem to be fighting yourself on every level, pulling yourself in two directions, always losing ground in both. I think you're so torn between your desire to be what you are and your need to cling to what you were that you're unable to accomplish anything."

Not the most flattering thing that anyone has said to me. "So you think I'm what? Neutralizing myself?"

"More like stalling your engine."

"Well, then." The wind off the ocean behind us is getting colder, and it cuts through my jacket. I don't let myself shiver. "Your theory doesn't solve anything though, does it? It's fine to say that I'm holding myself back and I should just be a vampire because I can't be human anymore, but that doesn't work for me. I've tried, believe me."

"I know."

I grind my teeth together, but I can't help spitting out my answer. "I *know* you know. You always seem to know everything, don't you?" I shouldn't be angry with him. Daniel has been more patient than I deserve, honing the skills I possess and helping me make up for the ones I'm lacking. Even at my lowest moments, Daniel has never let me believe that failure was an option.

My anger fades, if grudgingly. I have no right to be mad at anyone but myself.

He sips his cold coffee again and shoots me a sideways glance. "I do have an idea, if you're interested."

"Please."

"Let go of it."

"But I just said that I—"

"Shut up for five seconds, please. Let me finish." He doesn't sound angry. "I'm not saying to let go of your humanity. Obviously that isn't working. The fact remains that you do need to let go of thinking of yourself that way, because it's not what you are, and that's not going to change. But maybe you should stop fighting the rest of it. The empathy you feel for them. The way you still value their lives. Your instinctive reactions when you see them misused."

My stomach flutters. "But that's all wrong, isn't it?"

"I don't know anymore." He drains the dregs of his coffee and fiddles with the plastic lid, snapping it on and off the cup. "I've been a vampire for more than seventy years, and in that time I've accepted a certain view of the world. One that keeps us separate and safe. We can't get weepy over the fates of creatures we consume. But now I find myself wondering if we're not too quick to force everyone to think the same way." He curls his lower lip into his mouth and grasps the corner under one fang, letting it roll out slowly as he considers his words. He sighs. "I knew you were going to cause me trouble the moment I laid eyes on you, but I couldn't help myself."

It's my turn to raise an eyebrow. "You chose me? I sort of got the impression Trixie and I were punishment for something."

A low chuckle rises from deep in his chest. "Well, yes. My current position as mentor was a severe and insulting demotion, if a temporary one. I'm free as soon as I release the two of you onto an unsuspecting world. I had to take someone on, and Trixie was the top recommendation from the nurses. Eager to learn, if a bit of a smartass. But I looked through the files, I observed, and there was something about you that..." He trails off.

"Made you want to take on a challenge?"

He half-smiles toward the harbour. "Maybe that was it. I'm not sure. There's always been something different about you, a strength hiding below your outer weakness. I couldn't tell whether you were a damsel in distress or a danger to us all. Perhaps it's because a year in that place didn't break you or change you, even as you learned to accept what you were. Or maybe there's some small, weak part of me that craves that compassion you have. We don't see it much in vampires. And some of us lose our humanity so quickly that it becomes unnerving."

I want to bask in this for a minute, but I can't ignore his last comment. And I can't help thinking of dark vials and soundproof feeding chambers, of crushed consciences and quick acceptance. "Like Trixie?"

His jaw muscles tighten. "She's one of them, yes. She's doing just as well as her pre-death assessments indicated she would. She's finished her training, really. She has a lot to learn, but that will all come with experience. She's ready. She knows it, I know it. She's everything a vampire is supposed to be. She's settled into this existence like she never knew any other, and she has the skills to make her way high in our society. If she wants to hunt rogues, I suspect she'll be quite good at it."

I can't help the envy that twists my stomach. I have mysterious potential. She has everything. "So why did you tell her we're not ready? Did you include her in that statement to spare my feelings?"

"Aviva, have I ever done anything to spare your feelings?"

I snort. "Not that I'm aware of."

He looks uncomfortable for a moment, and then his expression shifts back to neutral. Unreadable. "I'm reluctant to let Trixie loose, so I hold on to both of you. There's just... something. It's as ineffable as whatever quality drew me to you, but completely different."

Silence follows, growing uncomfortable as the seconds pass.

"Trixie's great," I say, more to break the silence than anything. "She's not a monster or anything, if that's what you're thinking. I mean, not more than you or I. I'm not exactly comfortable with her wanting to taste pain and fear, but she's allowed to do that if the stock are willing, right? She's not doing anything wrong."

But that's a technicality. I want to defend her, but calling her behaviour anything close to *right* leaves a bitter taste in my mouth. Yes, the humans consent to it, but they do it to get the poison they're addicted to. Most of them don't want the type of terror and pain we offer in our little vials. Vampires like Trixie prey on the weak, the used up, the desperate, the ones who will do anything for their fix. Everyone's getting what they want in the end, but...

Daniel has been watching as I think it through. He's promised he can't see our thoughts, but mine are likely written all over my face. "It's complicated, isn't it?" He drums his fingers against the stone wall. "But you're correct. My assessment should have nothing to do with her preferences. Even the people she hurts have it better than they would in other times or places. But it occasionally concerns me how quickly she developed her tastes."

"It's not wrong, but it's not right," I say softly.

He frowns. "Something like that, but you might want to consider breaking the habit of thinking in those human terms."

I don't have an answer for that. I may have mostly accepted what I am, and figured out that what I once thought of as my spiritual place in the universe is no longer even a theoretical possibility... but I'm not prepared to walk away from all of my human morality just because I now belong to darkness, if I belong to anything at all.

"I'm keeping an eye on Trixie," Daniel says. "But I can't do it forever. It's unfair to her, anyway. As you rightly said, she's... great. She will live as she wishes within the laws of our society."

I have nothing to say to that. Trixie is my friend. My only friend, really. Daniel is too much of an authority figure for me to think of him that way, no matter how nice he's being to me right now. Definitely not someone I can go to with my personal problems. I tell him anything that's relevant to my training, but it's Trixie who I hang around with, who I share my space with, who I laugh so hard with that we snort drinks out of our noses. Talking about her this way feels like a betrayal.

"But I didn't come here to talk to you about Trixie," Daniel says. "What I wanted to say is that I think you might consider forgetting your focus on detachment from the living, at least for the time being. Accept who you are right now and let yourself move forward on other fronts. Seek the great potential I see in you."

I almost feel like I'm blushing. "Let myself be a shitty vampire in some ways so I can become better in others?"

Daniel tilts his chin upward, biting back a smile. "That's one way of looking at it, if you're going to insist on that ridiculous humility that clings to you so unflatteringly."

Can I do that? All he's suggesting is that I accept this amazing thing that I am, embracing my power without letting its darker implications hold me back. I was human once, and still hold those emotions and memories, but I'm so much more now. I know that, and feel it to my very core when I feed. Can I embrace that if it means I don't have to lose myself?

I nod. "Let's see if just thinking that way makes any difference. Give me a minute, then sneak up on me."

He rolls his eyes. "Not sure whether it counts if you know I'm coming. Close your eyes. I may or may not be back."

He stands and drops off the edge of the tower like it was a low garden wall. A loud thwack echoes out as his shoes hit the ground, but any movements that follow are silent. I close my eyes and scent the night air, trying to catch a hint of him, but all I get is the salty air of this place that's starting to feel like home. My body is perfectly still, without even a heartbeat to distract my ears. The sounds of the city drift across the harbour.

I have no idea where Daniel might be until I hear the sharp rap of a knuckle against a car window. "Leave room for the Holy Spirit, children," he warns.

I giggle. I'd nearly forgotten about the teenagers below.

So that places Daniel a short jog down a slight slope to my right, downwind. I won't hear or smell him.

I climb up to the top of the tower and turn my focus

inward, ignoring the senses I rely too heavily on. I am more than them. I feel for Daniel with a part of me that runs deeper than my physical being—a part that exists within the black core of my new nature. I let the darkness wash over me. I am still Aviva. I am still me. And I am more. I let my awareness flow out of me.

And I feel something. A dark flame flickering in the night. Daniel.

As soon as I feel it, he's gone. But it was there.

Fine. If he's going to play tricks, I'll use the ones he's taught me. In the past, he's asked me to play with the idea of sensing intentions rather than presences. It's still difficult, especially with someone like Daniel who often seems not to possess them. I've never had much luck with it, myself, but I'm willing to give it another try.

Instead of searching for my trainer himself, I search for the part of him that wants to harm me. And instead of the desperate, wild seeking that I usually manage, I start my search from a deeper place. A calmer one. A place that feels ancient, though it's the newest part of me, and powerful enough that I have been terrified of losing myself in it.

But I won't be lost. I won't be changed.

There.

Malicious intent approaches, climbing the wall behind me, clearer than I've ever felt anything from another vampire. A hot red desire to see me defeated, torn down, begging for mercy.

Not this time. When he strikes out, I'm ready. I tuck into a tight roll and spring back to my feet just before I go over the edge. He doesn't pursue, and the malice fades. He's pleased, but I lose my sense of that when I open my eyes.

I press my lips together, holding back my excitement. This shouldn't be a huge deal, but for me it is. I've never accessed my power like this. Never felt anything beyond my senses so clearly.

"Good," he says. "Too easy, but good."

That's about as open as Daniel ever gets with praise during training, so I'm satisfied. "You're right, too easy," I say, flipping my hair back and resting a hand on my hip. "It would be far more challenging if I had a trainer who didn't actually want to maim and destroy me."

He smirks. "Aww. Does that hurt your feelings? Chin up. What doesn't kill you makes you stronger, and all of that."

"Well, Daniel, I'm already dead. Does that make me invincible, or hopelessly weak?"

"Moot point. Let's do it again. I'll make it harder for you."

I chuckle at the unintentional innuendo, and he shoots me a dark glower.

I position myself in the centre of the roof, and he disappears completely. I can't catch a flicker of him, not even the slightest hint of his irritation.

He's not going to go easy on me. The thought is thrilling, in a strange way. The fact that he's willing to hurt me means he knows I'm strong enough to handle it. I retreat deeper into my darkest heart, waiting for what I felt before. Even if he changes his plan of attack, his intention will feel the same, and even if he's more careful to mask it, I should sense *something*. Whether he plans to kick, punch, grab me by my hair, throw me over—

Cold lips press against mine, and iron-strong arms pull my shocked body close. Long fingers tangle in my hair.

My mind explodes in confusion. I should pull away, fight him off, but my body betrays me completely. My mouth opens under his, and the most incredible energy washes over me as I rise up on my toes and push myself harder against him. It's not like the feeling I get from feeding, but another kind of awakening entirely. His venom gives his tongue a sharp flavour that sends desire coursing through me like I haven't experienced since I was alive, lighting me up from within. The world around us stops moving.

And then he's gone, pulling back, leaving me to stumble forward into the space where he stood a moment ago.

He's got a cocky grin plastered across his face as he runs his tongue over his fangs. "Your methods are flawed, dear student. I told you that you assume too much about me."

"That wasn't fair!" It's all I can do not to stomp my foot in a childish fit of confusion and anger. "And pointless for training. No one who wants to hurt me is going to sneak up and *kiss* me."

"No?" I barely dodge a kick that would have sent me over the edge of the tower again. "Well, there's your lesson for tonight."

"What? Expect the unexpected? That's original." Am I sulking? I hope not.

"No. But be open to possibilities outside of your expectations, and look outside of what I've taught you." He thinks for a moment, studying me as his smile fades. "And know that if you give away your methods and your gifts, you invite enemies to find ways around them. I shouldn't have known how you sensed me. You're too trusting. Does that lesson suit you better?"

Absolutely nothing suits me better right now, and nothing will until I have time alone to smooth my ruffled feathers. I'm still trying to pick bits of my shattered mind out of the air they're floating in. I can't let him see that, though. Maybe he knows anyway. Of course, he seems fine. Cool and unaffected by whatever he tasted in me.

Well, fuck him. Fuck him and his stupid gorgeous body and his ridiculously good kiss.

I straighten my jacket. "That's fine, thank you. Was there anything else?"

He shoves his hands in his pockets and gives me a slow smile. "No, that should do for tonight. You want to go home?"

"Please."

We don't speak on the drive back. At first Daniel seems pleased to have gotten to me, but then I get the feeling he wants to ask whether I'm angry.

I don't reassure him. Let him be confused for a while. Misery loves company.

———————

CHAPTER TEN

Trixie shrieks as she flies off the edge of the concrete bunker and lets out a loud "oof" as she hits the gun platform below.

She giggles. "Viva! Look at you!"

I can't help the wide grin that spreads across my face, even as Daniel shoots Trixie a dark look for her delight over her own defeat. We're supposed to be acting like this is actual combat, testing my improved perceptions on a dark night at Cape Spear. We're taking it seriously, but Daniel must be out of his mind if he expects us to take all of this in stride.

We're dead, after all, not *dead*.

It's only been a few days since my last training session with Daniel, but I've come far thanks to his permission to stop trying so damn hard. Not that I don't still have a long way to go, but I'm feeling it. I'm digging deep, accessing a part of myself I was only aware of in the vaguest terms. I'm finding strength that goes deeper than my muscles, sensing things I wouldn't have noticed a week ago. I'm more than a match for Daniel's star student now.

If only I could tell her why. That part still hurts. Daniel's hinted that I should keep anything relating to my feelings toward the living to myself. He hasn't come right out and said it, but I've figured out that to let on I still care about them could be more than social suicide. Daniel didn't just shut me down at that crime scene because he was embarrassed. He was protecting me.

Vampire culture is built not just on rules, but on appearances, unwritten expectations, and above all, a strict separation from our prey. We can partake of their culture as long as it doesn't affect us. We can avail ourselves of their technology, as long as it doesn't harm us or complicate our separation. We can go to the movies or watch TV if we don't find wearing eye protection too annoying; we can read their books and listen to their music. But we cannot interact with them on a personal level, and we cannot *care*.

To disobey the unwritten rules of the clan would be to make myself a danger to it. Not in the same way as the rogues are, but...

But I need to watch my ass. Trixie knows I've made strides in connecting with my vampiric nature, but she thinks it's because I've taken her advice to heart.

I take a deep breath of the air whipping in from off the

ocean, relishing the strength that flows through my aching muscles even as I ignore Daniel's searching glance.

I've been ignoring those since the night he kissed me.

I feel like a goddess, and I haven't even fed tonight. This is what it's supposed to be like. My old life is over, but I am still here. I feed on the living, but I was re-born into a world where we don't have to kill, where we protect our stock. And if our motivations for doing so are selfish, well... maybe doing the right thing for the wrong reasons isn't so bad. Maybe being a vampire isn't the worst fate.

I end that train of thought before it enters the deep tunnel that takes me back to the little white church.

That severed spiritual connection is a deep wound, but one I finally feel might heal in time. Becoming a vampire wasn't my choice, but no angel swooped in to save me from this fate. And tonight, with the wonder of my new being coursing through me, with the cliffs and lighthouse and white picket fences that surround me picked out in stark relief even in the dark, with the stars spilling over me like a glittering blanket that I could wrap around myself if I cared to reach out and embrace it, I feel whole for the first time. Complete in myself and my nighttime world.

The light doesn't want me now. Perhaps it is time to embrace the darkness. I can live in this world without hurting anyone. I can hunt those who do, help protect the living for my own reasons. No one needs to know what those are.

A double life isn't ideal, but for now, it's better than nothing.

I'm about to jump down to help Trixie up when Daniel approaches. "You're doing well."

"Thank you. I'm feeling better about a lot of things."

"Good. About the other—"

His phone rings, cutting him off. He seems about to ignore it, then frowns and flips it open. "Yes?"

He wanders away, not motioning for me to wait for him, but I do. Trixie walks up the side of the grassy hill to stand with me.

"What's up with you two?" she asks. "Everything's been weird since you had your breakthrough. He's not giving you shit for something, is he?"

"No. It's fine."

It is fine. It's not like I've been thinking about his kiss the way I usually think about blood. Or like I'm suddenly considering what he'd be like in bed. I haven't cared much about sex since I died—not as a separate thing from the pure joy of feeding, at least. But now I'm wondering whether a guy with no pulse can get it up, whether he fucks like he fights.

I need to get over this. Vampires don't have relationships. Alliances, yes. Friendships, yeah... as long as they don't get too mushy or require unrepayable sacrifice. But not romance. And I feel too close to human to trust myself not to get swoony if I let myself want him too badly.

"Viva?"

"It's fine, Trixie. We talked about some hard stuff, we trained, I had a breakthrough. Maybe it's just weird because I'm starting to feel like it would be okay to not train under him anymore."

She purses her lips and nods. "That's fair. I was starting to wonder whether you might be wanting to do other things under him."

Daniel is back before I can formulate a response to that. He frowns at us.

"You don't have to come out for this one."

Trixie perks up. "Another body?"

"Yes, but not connected to the rogues. One of our stock. Miranda just wants me to check it over to make sure it's nothing that will be traced back to us."

My stomach plummets, but I don't offer a comment. Instead I ask, "How did they die?"

"That's one of the questions we need to answer before we release her to human authorities. You two keep working here. I'll be back to pick you up soon."

But he doesn't object when we follow him back to the car.

The drive down the long, winding road back to town would be peaceful if I wasn't feeling my old anxieties creeping back. It's fine. People die. That's the only guarantee in life, isn't it? Our stock aren't exempt. And this will be a good time to test my reaction to a body now that I'm not fighting with myself. I don't have to deny my reactions. Just hide them.

No problem.

St. John's isn't a city of high-rise apartments, but mid-level buildings dot its landscape, providing affordable housing for much of the population. A male vampire in blue jeans and a plaid shirt meets us at the door of a white building and leads us up to the fourth floor. The smell of cooking cabbage wafts out from one of the doors we pass, and the sickly, skunky smell of pot from another. A baby cries down the hall.

Sometimes I forget that the living occupy the night just as we do. The humans who live here can't experience all of this activity as clearly as I do, but I wonder what it's like to live in a building where people are so closely connected to the intimate details of their neighbours' lives. Will these people care that their neighbour is gone? Did they ever wonder where she went so many nights?

The other vampire leaves us without a word at the door to the apartment and heads back downstairs. I guess we're not the only troops Miranda has called in tonight.

Daniel leads us to the bathroom, then pauses in the doorway. His shoulders drop. Just slightly, for the briefest moment. To a living eye it might have seemed nothing more than an inconsequential shiver, but I catch it. He steps in and reaches for a tissue to guard his fingers before he picks up one of the two empty prescription bottles on the counter. Several boxes of over-the-counter sleeping pills are scattered around as well, blister packs exposed and empty.

Our victim—if that's what she is—lies in the bathtub. If the water was hot enough to steam up the mirror when she ran the bath, that heat is gone now. The room holds the chill of a tomb. Appropriate enough, given the lack of heartbeat among the four of us.

I turn to Trixie. She looks a little green.

I'm not going to ask. It's not my business, any more than my freak-out at the murder scene was hers.

I look instead to the victim. She's clothed in jeans and a tight white tank top that shows off both her petite frame and the faint scars on her neck. The wounds we leave tend to heal up quickly, a process aided by flavourless compounds in the little vials we offer our stock. Still, after a few visits, we leave our marks on them. This was certainly one of ours. She stares wide-eyed at the ceiling.

Vomit floats on the surface of the filthy water and coats her chin. No blood. There's an empty bottle of bottom-shelf vodka on the floor, though.

Daniel leans back against the little counter beside the toilet and folds his arms across his chest. He's rolled up the sleeves of his white shirt to the elbows, but I'm in no mood to admire his well-muscled forearms. "Well, crew?"

"Suicide," I whisper. My throat closes. It's not the how that bothers me, but the why.

Trixie clears her throat. "I'd guess she took the pills over a decent time frame. Got the drugs deep into her system before she could pass out. Drank to make sure they'd do their job. Got into the tub so she'd drown if they didn't, but asphyxiated first."

"Should we consider foul play?" I ask, feeling like I've suddenly fallen into a crime show on TV.

Daniel shakes his head. "No. This is not unprecedented."

I look at the victim again. Small. Pretty. Like Daniel likes them. I glance at him and catch the tightness around his eyes.

"She's the one who freaked out the other night, isn't she?"

He rubs a hand over his jaw. "She is." The apartment's door opens on squeaky hinges. He glances out, motions for someone to come in, and looks back to the body. "It happens when they can't move past the addiction."

My skin crawls. We did this. Not directly, but if not for us, if not for our club where we're so careful to treat them decently and not kill them, she'd be alive.

I step out into the hallway to give myself some space as the most beautiful vampire I've ever seen strides toward us. And that's saying something. Many of us have faces that leave human beauty in the dust, but this one must have had angels for parents. She moves with long strides, hips moving like she's wearing heels even though her black boots are as flat as mine. Silver hair streams behind her, long enough to graze the bottom hem of her black suit jacket. It's a stunning contrast to her unlined face. Were she alive, I'd place her at a perfectly maintained forty years old. Given the dark depths of her cobalt eyes, I'm going to guess that she's been dead nearly as long as Miranda.

A big male vampire is now waiting by the door, arms crossed over his chest, scowling at us. Or maybe that's just his face. Not everyone is born with the potential for perfection. His bald head shines under the overhead lights, and thick eyebrows shadow small, dark eyes.

I step backward to give the female space to enter the little bathroom. She assesses the scene, then nods to Daniel. "Good to see you again."

He lowers his gaze. "A pleasure as always, Katya."

Trixie squeezes out of the bathroom, but her eyes don't leave the newcomer. I can't look away, either. Her power is quiet and controlled, but it's undeniable. Either she can't conceal hers like Daniel can, or she wants to make an impression on the new kids. I wonder if that's common among elders—and there's no question that's what she is. One of the old ones, the great powers who built our world.

"Nothing unexpected?" she asks. Her voice is silk, silvery and smooth as her hair.

"I don't think so." Daniel doesn't sound broken up by this. That's as it should be for a vampire, but his indifference is off-putting. The life that once flowed in the dead woman could well still be in him, yet for all I can tell she could be a complete stranger. "We'll make sure there's no note of her scars on the autopsy report, but otherwise there's nothing that should concern us. Looks like she lived alone."

"Excellent."

"When did you get back from London?"

I leave their conversation behind to head for the bedroom and push the flimsy wooden door open. The white walls are unadorned save for a couple of band posters held up with blue putty. Someone's landlord must have been a real treat to deal with. The bed's made, everything tidied up. A few bright scarves hang over the mirror on the dresser.

I sink down on the edge of the bed and close my eyes. It's quiet here. No shadows. I'm not freaking out this time.

At least that's something to be thankful for. But as I look around, I realize how little I've thought about our stock. Who they are outside the club.

How did she get there and home? Did her visits to the club affect her daily life, her job?

Not once have I wondered like this about any of them. I've never asked their names. I've seen them as less than human within the club's walls, and never even realized it. I've cared that they were there by choice, that they wouldn't suffer permanent harm. Or so I thought.

But when I've been there to feed, they've only been my prey.

It seems wrong that I have the audacity to care about this one now, or about the victims at the crime scene. I rise and move toward the mirror. It's a myth that we don't have reflections. I can see myself clearly now. Pale skin displaying the weakness of my blood, pale eyes betraying how new I am to all of this. I lean on the edge of the dresser and press my forehead to the glass, inhaling the perfume that clings to the scarves.

A shadow flickers in front of me when I close my eyes, as though reflected in the mirror. Fainter than the ones at the crime scene, and silent. I hold still, focusing. It's gone... but I wonder.

This isn't a freak-out. I don't feel like I'm going insane, but the shadows are back.

Trixie's and Katya's voices move down the hallway toward the open-concept kitchen and living room at the other end of the short hallway. I walk silently back to the bathroom, assuming Daniel is with them.

He's not. He's still standing there, looking down at her.

I touch the bare skin of his forearm. "You okay?"

"Of course." But his voice catches.

"Daniel."

He smiles sadly at me. "We have to be okay. Understand?"

"I remember." It's a relief to know he feels something. I

look down at her. "Can I have a minute alone here? I want to try something."

"Absolutely. Just don't disturb anything. I'll be with the others."

He's almost out the door when he turns back, reaches down toward her face, and closes her eyes, resting his hand there for a moment before lifting it, then wiping any trace of himself away with a damp cloth. She looks peaceful now. Not like the rogues' victims.

Daniel leans in close on his way by me so that his breath tickles my ear when he speaks. "Not a word to anyone about that, Aviva."

I almost smile. "I'll assume it was for my benefit."

"Very good."

And maybe it was. If I caught the slump of his shoulders when he identified the victim, he surely caught my despair as I did the same. Maybe he did this for me, so I wouldn't have to struggle with the decision of whether to let myself do it. But maybe he did it for her.

The more I learn about my new world, the less I know.

I close the door behind him. It should feel strange to be alone with a corpse. Creepy. But she's not bad company, really, as long as I don't breathe in the smells her death left lingering in the air.

I sit on the closed lid of the toilet and close my eyes again. I reach for the darkness in me, my deepest power, and feel nothing unexpected. No shadows. No ghosts here.

And yet I still wonder whether there's a chance that the shadows aren't my mind playing horrible tricks, but something else.

The shadows came at the other house when I opened myself to seeing the victims as people, when I let my human emotions take over. I think back to the bright scarves, the perfume. I think of the thin walls and the nights she likely spent trying to sleep while the neighbour's baby cried and kept her awake. I think of her open, staring eyes, and the darkness. Not the one that fills me. Mine is an active darkness, a void that's somehow full to bursting with potential. Instead I think of the darkness that led her here, to a pile of drugs and a cheap bottle of alcohol, to a tub where the skin on her fingertips wrinkled as she died choking on her own vomit instead of slipping off to sleep as she likely expected.

The loss she endured, one she couldn't even remember after the Inferno's enforcers wiped her memory.

A cool tear slips down the side of my nose as I stand and turn toward the counter without opening my eyes.

A shadow passes in front of me. Faint, disappearing as it passes the edge of the mirror's frame. It's not as present as those at the crime scene. Just an impression of movement, and a faint wave of despair that tightens around my heart and tugs. No fear. In fact, there's something like hope buried in the pain.

I open my eyes, and it's gone.

"I hope you found the peace you wanted," I tell her softly. Not that I think she's around to hear it.

I don't know why this shadow was softer. Maybe because she didn't die in terror like the others. Maybe only murder leaves such strong impressions, or maybe it's vampire involvement that strengthens them. But I'm grateful to her.

I understand now. I wasn't losing my mind when I got caught up in the screaming, swirling darkness in that kitchen.

Daniel was right about me. My potential goes deeper than either of us understood, and it's connected to my empathy. I just wish I knew what it meant for the investigation.

When I join the others in the living room, Trixie is listening raptly as Katya tells Daniel a story about the vampires of London. Katya's bodyguard is sitting on a hard chair by the dining room table, hunched over with his elbows resting on his knees, shooting cold glances at Daniel.

Katya smiles at me, cool and confident. "And you're Aviva. I've heard about you."

I'm not sure how to take that. So much depends on who she's spoken to. "Miranda mentioned you to me, as well," I say, glad I at least have that. I may have my faults, but my memory has improved since I died, and I remember every word of that conversation in the club. "She must be glad you've returned."

Katya's smile widens. "It seems like things are quite under control, but we're happy to be here to help, aren't we, Christopher?"

Her grumpy friend nods reluctantly.

She looks around the shabby living room. "Not here specifically, of course. I think we're finished, Daniel?"

"Absolutely."

We take the stairs down. It's not until we reach the car that I realize Trixie and Katya have fallen behind.

"Hold on. They'll be a minute," Christopher grumbles, and heads for a white car at the end of the parking lot.

Katya approaches us a minute later, Trixie trailing a few paces behind.

Daniel gives her a wry smile. "Stealing her, are you?"

Katya chuckles. "You know she's suited to this work, and ready for far more than what she's doing now. You've been good for her, but she could be learning more from a new teacher." She glances back at Trixie, who has stopped far enough back to give them room to talk in private. Katya drops her voice to a murmur. "She respects you, Daniel, but she's overconfident and too familiar with you to want to listen. You know me well enough to know I'll steer her right."

"She's all yours." He says it loud enough that Trixie can hear, and she lets out a little squeak. He seems relieved. I guess he sees this as better than letting her loose on her own. "Where are you staying?"

"The usual place downtown. I'll get her a room. There's no point setting her up anywhere permanent if she'll be travelling with me."

My stomach drops. "She's moving out?"

Katya smiles at me. "Don't worry, little one. He'll turn you out of the nest soon enough." She steps back and looks us over, as though framing us for a portrait. She laughs, revealing her fangs. "Or maybe he's just been waiting to get you alone." She strides away before either of us can answer. "Trixie will be by for her things shortly," she calls back over her shoulder.

"Elders think they're so fucking smart," Daniel grumbles, and gets behind the wheel of the car.

As soon as my limbs unfreeze, I take my place beside him.

The memory of the body upstairs fades as the understanding of what's just happened hits me.

Trixie is moving out.

I'm going to be living alone with Daniel.

Shit.

CHAPTER ELEVEN

T rixie is gone.

It took us all night to get her things packed. I expected her to take some clothes and cosmetics, things you'd take on any little trip, and come back for the rest when she needed it. Instead, she took it all. Not that we own a lot, mind you. Most of what's in the house is Daniel's. But her room is empty save for the furniture. It looks like an empty dorm room.

She's really not coming back.

I'm exhausted. Packing up her shit wasn't physically tiring like training was earlier tonight, or as mentally taxing as our brief investigation of the suicide, but I'm emotionally drained. Everything changed tonight. I want to go to bed and sleep the day away, but I'll have to pass the open door of her room to get to mine, and that's the most exhausting thought of all.

Instead I sit on the kitchen counter, in the spot Trixie's big, fancy coffeemaker used to occupy. I don't know why she would need that at the hotel where she's staying, but it's gone. Daniel prowls around the room, opening and closing cupboards. Checking to see if she missed anything, I guess, but we don't keep a lot in here. There's not much need for gourmet cooking equipment when you feed on the living.

He glances at me, opens his mouth, and closes it, shaking his head.

I understand. I feel like there are things I should be saying, questions I should be asking, but the words aren't making it from my brain to my mouth.

I feel like my heart should be pounding as I watch him. My body is certainly responding in other ways. There's no doubting what I'm feeling now, what I want now that we're alone.

My own body is still a mystery to me. I'm not allowed to know all our secrets. The living have speculated for so long about us that there are a thousand theories and superstitions ranging from horrifying to downright twee, but the reality is stranger than all of it.

I'm dead. And I'm aware. A few hours ago I was shut in a bathroom with a corpse, reflecting on my own culpability in her death, and now all my mind wants to focus on is how Daniel's body moves beneath his clothes, lean and strong and predatory. Maybe I am a monster, if I can move on so quickly.

I should ask him if he's all right. Something back in that apartment affected him, I know it did. But I also know he won't talk about it. We're not supposed to, and Daniel is nothing if not faithful to the rules.

He looks at me again. My skin prickles as his gaze locks on mine, then trails slowly down my body. I've already changed into my pyjamas. The oversized pants are modest enough, but the tight top doesn't hide much, and I don't need to look down to know it's obvious where my thoughts have wandered.

Does he feel the same about me? Katya seemed to think so, but aside from that one kiss that could just have been about teaching me a lesson...

Fuck it. I have no idea. All I know is that I want him. Maybe I always have, but was too scared to realize it. Too respectful. Too distracted by trying to find my place in this new world.

He steps closer, cold hazel eyes shadowed by thick brows drawn together in a concerned frown. "You did well tonight," he says. I told him about the shadows on the drive back. He didn't have much to say about them, but he seemed pleased that I'd got something. "Your training with Trixie, the body. You seemed okay with it."

"Not okay. Just... better."

He smiles sadly and looks down. "You do get used to it."

"Daniel?"

"Hmm?"

"I'm sorry I was so cold toward you the past few days. Since our last training session."

He meets my gaze again. "Was it because I kissed you?"

Direct. There's nothing coy about Daniel, at least not as I know him. I like that. It's not like I can trust just anyone these days, but I do trust him. He's never intentionally misled me. Always tried to help my helpless ass even when it was the last job in the world he wanted to be doing.

I really am sorry I pushed him away when we finally made progress.

"It was the kiss, yeah. I just..." Something tugs at my cold, still heart. I'm more nervous now than I was heading to that crime scene in Kilbride. "It confused me. I tried not to look at you that way, you know? You're like a teacher, and I'm a good student."

The corners of his eyes crinkle as he holds back a smile. "You are that. So you think it was wrong of me to offer that lesson?"

"No. I mean, I still say it was a dirty trick, but I... And you were..." My thoughts are as flustered as they were that night, ready to blow away on the breeze coming in through the half-open window. I clear my throat to give myself a second to pull them together. "Anyway, I didn't want to tell you that you got to me. Didn't want to give you the satisfaction. But I guess it was obvious."

He raises an eyebrow and lets that smile loose. I shift uncomfortably on my hard seat as he steps closer again. "Your response was most gratifying in the moment." The smile fades. "I did question the decision after, a hundred times. I didn't mean to confuse you or push you away." He reaches over to close the window, then pushes his hair back with one hand and lets the strands fall over his eyes. "I can't train you anymore, Aviva. We're done."

"What? Daniel, no. I still respect you, I swear. Nothing has changed." He can't kick me out. "I admit that since that night I've had thoughts I shouldn't, and that's your fault. But it will be fine. I can control myself. Nothing has to change."

He takes another step closer and rests his hands on the counter on either side of me. "I hope that's not true."

He's close enough that the scent of his skin fills me even if I'm not breathing him in. So unlike a living man. Stronger. Darker. Colder. I grip the edge of the counter hard enough that I feel like the Formica might snap in my grasp, not sure why I feel like I have to fight the desire that washes over me in warm waves. Maybe it's because I paid a high price for this desire when I was alive, when my questions and my needs ended with me being outcast from my group of friends in a little white church when I needed them the most.

I'm not going to think about my old life. Daniel was right. The rights and wrongs of the living aren't mine now. Not here. Not tonight. If Daniel wants me and I want him, that's all there is.

We answer to no one.

He leans in. "Say I'm not your trainer anymore."

The silence stretches out between us, delicious tension that I want to shatter into a million pieces. I don't move. I can't. But I can speak.

"You're not my trainer anym—"

Daniel's mouth cuts off my words, pressing harder than the other night, forcing my lips against my teeth. I draw a sharp breath as he pulls back, leaving a hair's breadth of space between us.

My move.

I don't hesitate now, reaching for the front of his shirt to pull his body against mine, running my hands over the hard curves and planes hidden beneath the cloth as our lips meet again. His tongue traces my lower lip and I relax my jaw, inviting him in. He tastes as sharp and poisonous as he did before, but now I have time to luxuriate in the sensation of his venom waking me up.

This isn't the same as the lust I felt when I was alive. This is darker, purer, flawless as a perfect diamond and just as sharp. The temperature of his body matches my own, eliminating the reminder of how *other* I am.

He twists his right hand through the hair above my neck, tilting my face fully toward his, and I willingly relax in his grip. It's been too long since I was kissed by anyone whose strength was more than a match for mine. There's a part of me that wants to fight him, to test him, but not yet.

This is too perfect.

I wrap my legs tight around his waist as he pulls my hips closer with his left arm, forcing me off balance. The fingers that were tangled in my hair trail down my throat, over my collarbone, and trace a circle around the outer curve of my left breast. I groan and twist, trying to catch his touch more fully, and he laughs as he pulls his face away from mine to trail his lips and tongue over my throat.

He's moving slowly, with a patience he's developed over a century of life and death, though it's now quite obvious that he could, in fact, just take me if he wanted to. If only I had the same experience to draw on. My impatience is almost as strong as the desire that burns hot as a furnace through my core. His cool touch is somehow melting me, and he hasn't so much as slipped a hand up my shirt. Every flicker of his tongue over my skin pushes me closer to throwing him to the floor and tearing his clothes off.

And then he bites me.

Just a nip on my collarbone, a faint spike of pain

followed by the caress of his lips. Enough to break my skin, to introduce his venom to my blood. The pleasure of it spreads slowly, fading in seconds, and I finally understand what keeps the living coming back to our little club.

"More," I whisper, and pull his face up to mine again. I bite his lower lip, and a low growl rises in his throat.

He grabs my wrist, forcing my hand against the surface of the cupboard behind me. He watches me for a moment, leans in and inhales deeply. "We shouldn't be doing this," he murmurs into my ear. "But I swear by the void, you're the most delicious thing I've ever set eyes on."

I don't ask why we shouldn't. If this is wrong, I don't want to know it. I just want him. I want his body, his pain, his poison. Everything.

I break free of his grasp and wrap my arms around his neck. I don't have the words to tell him that no one has ever made me feel as alive as I do at this moment. Heartbeat or no, something brighter and wilder than the divine spark that once filled me flows through my veins. I want to pull back, to look at him and feast on the perfect lines of his jaw, to lose myself in his eyes, but I can't. The need to feel him is too strong.

He lifts me from the counter and carries me out of the kitchen and up the stairs as though my muscular frame weighs nothing. By the time we reach the landing, I've got his shirt open. I shove it back off his shoulders and let one hand roam over his pale skin as the other holds me close to him.

He's about to make the turn to go up the next flight when I tug on his arm, directing him to my room.

"Too far," I whisper, and bite his earlobe.

He doesn't argue.

It's still technically dark outside, but dawn is threatening. The faint, murky light that shows between my half-opened curtains is more than enough to bring out all of the details in the room, but all I can see is Daniel. He fills my senses, and I feel his desire reflecting my own, doubling it the way a mirror near a window will make a room brighter. He's not shielding himself, and for the first time the full force of his dark, raw power becomes real to me.

If Trixie had ever sensed this, she wouldn't have had the nerve to talk back to him. My mouth goes dry and my chest tightens. I'm afraid of him. I'd be a fool not to be. But it changes nothing.

Daniel and I drop to the bed together. He catches himself on his hands before he crushes me, but the distance between our bodies remains constant, pressed together at the hips, room enough between our upper bodies for our hands to move. I can't decide whether I want to focus on the sensations of him touching me or the gorgeous feel of his body under my own hands. It's overwhelming, every bit of it.

He tugs at the bottom of my top, and I arch my back so

he can pull it over my head, revealing my bare skin beneath. He groans softly and kisses me again as one hand cups my breast, his thumb finally grazing my nipple and sending a lightning bolt of pleasure directly between my thighs.

One hand. He's using the other to support himself. I need more. I push his shoulder hard enough that he gets the message, and we roll together to trade positions. I straddle his hips, grinding against him, frustrated by how much clothing we're still wearing and yet revelling in the delay. We only get this delicious first-time torture once. I know I should draw it out, but his hands are now freely exploring my body, and his expert touch combined with the seductive weight of his power is driving me mad.

He judges my reactions, adjusting his touch to every shift and moan, offering me pleasure I couldn't have imagined with a living man. It's perfect.

I don't want perfect. I want the Daniel I know, the one who's bruised me and broken me. The one I need to see made weak by his desire for me.

I lean forward, brushing my tits over his gorgeous chest, and sink my fangs deep into his shoulder.

Vampire blood is weak, and I won't get any energy from him. But I get what I want. He gasps, then snarls and rolls over, pinning me under him. My fangs tear long, jagged stripes in his flesh as he arches away from me, and pale blood flows down over his chest.

He leans in close again, pressing his own fangs danger-ously close to my throat, then brushes his lips against my ear. "Is that how it's going to be, then?"

My heart's not beating, but I feel it—the rush of fear washing over my skin, the high tension in my chest. I'm playing with fire, and it's so fucking hot I can't stand it. I want to be able to use my body in ways I can't with fragile living men. I want to fight with Daniel and bring the battle to the conclusion I now understand I've always wanted.

I dig my nails into his back and move my hips beneath him. He's impossibly hard.

"Just fuck me." It's hoarse, but I've found my voice at last.

He stands and undoes his belt.

Beauty is a nearly worthless currency among vampires, and I've been around them long enough that I should be numb to it by now. Daniel, however, is something different tonight. Every curve of muscle stands out in the pre-dawn light, every perfect inch visible as he drops his trousers to the floor and steps toward the bed. His hair falls forward again, shadowing his eyes as a devilish grin reveals fangs I'd kill to feel piercing my skin again.

I'm glad I never let myself imagine this moment before. I never would have got it right.

He bends toward me for long enough to grab my pants and pull them off in one smooth motion, then drops on top of me again, one knee pressing against my inner thigh, pushing my legs open. I'm not going to fight him on that. I ache for him, and it's all I can do to keep from screaming at him to take me.

My senses are as strong as they've ever been, yet everything is a blur. Daniel is touching me, kissing my body, exploring, and every sensation weaves itself into a web of pure pleasure and lust. I'm trying to keep up, running my hands over his body, tearing at him with my nails when he sinks his fangs into the skin below my collarbone, sending another pulse of poison into me.

I wrap my legs around the backs of his thighs, urging him closer. He positions himself over me, and I shudder hard as he slides in.

It was never this good when I was alive. Never this pure. Never this free of guilt and consequence.

Our bodies grow warmer as we move together. I want to draw this out, but I've lost any chance at self-control. Pleasure washes over me in waves, and I'm falling into a sea of sunlight that goes on forever. I try to keep my cries quiet enough that the neighbours won't call the cops, but it's a battle I can't win. Daniel buries his face against my neck and groans, shuddering against me, pushing deeper and harder as he reaches the height of his own pleasure, urging me over the edge with him.

And then everything is still save for the quaking of our muscles as we lie tangled up with each other. After a moment, Daniel rolls over, pulling me with him, unwilling to let go.

That's fine by me. I could lie with him forever, world be damned.

And this, I realize, is the danger of what we've just done.

CHAPTER TWELVE

W e may have spent the day in bed, but we sure as hell didn't get much sleeping done.

"So let me just make sure I have this a hundred percent right," I say, trailing my nails gently over Daniel's chest and down his stomach. He shivers. "We can fuck as much as we want, but no icky relationship stuff? No goopy-schmoopy valentines? No declarations of undying—"

He flips me on my back and plants a deep kiss on me that curls my toes. I had no idea that was a thing that could actually happen. "None of that." He stretches out on his side, bedsheet draped over his waist just low enough to tease. Not that I haven't spent the day exploring what's under there, but I could go for another look. "You knew this."

It's almost a question. "I did." I lean in and nip his shoulder gently. "I was asking for a friend."

"Hmm."

"But why?" Before he can answer, I say, "Not that it's a problem. I mean, you're a good lay and all, but hardly marriage material. I'm just curious."

His mouth quirks sideways. "That's a relief." He thinks for a minute, staring up at the ceiling. "I think you know the simple answer. And I don't think you really want more than that."

The simple answer is that we're not meant to form alliances. It's every vampire for him- or herself in our world, even within our strict cooperative social structure. We have our hierarchy. We respect the elders and obey them. We have social relationships. Even friendships. But nothing deep enough that we might be tempted to do anything stupid in the name of affection or loyalty. Ideally, at least.

And I've never heard of vampires in a romantic relationship. I'm guessing there's more sex than I ever suspected, but maybe we grow out of that need in time, too.

There's more, though. There's that thing Daniel has hinted at when he's suggested I leave my past as far behind me as I can.

He looks at me, brow furrowed with concern. "You're still so close to everything we leave behind. And I..." He reaches out and tucks a loose lock of my hair behind my ear. "I find that appealing. That may be why I haven't been forcing you forward, and perhaps that's unfair to you."

A chill flashes over my bare skin. "I'm ready. I think, in a weird way, being allowed to acknowledge my connection to all of that has helped me understand what it means to be a vampire. The darkness inside of me..." I chew my lip as I pull my thoughts together. "That's what we have instead of life, isn't it?"

He nods. "It's not such a bad thing, right?"

"But?"

His fingers brush over my brow and trail down my face, skimming my eyelashes and my lips. Soft, like the touch of a fairy's wings. So unlike the Daniel I saw early this morning. "But, dear Aviva. To crave love or anything like it is to chase something that you and I are no longer a part of. When you changed, the light rejected you. Daylight burns you. If you were to enter a church or a mosque or a temple, you would grow weak and feel its atmosphere crushing you to dust."

"God is love," I whisper, parroting back the Sunday school lesson I clung to when His people rejected me. Even when I left the church, I held onto that. I was still His. Still loved.

Daniel cups my jaw in his hand, lifting my face so I look at him. "That's a simple human way of looking at it. You were deep in the light when you lived, Aviva. That's why you never should have been chosen for this. It makes the transition too hard. But you need to understand this. We are creatures of the void."

I force a smile. "Not children of the spiky-tailed devil?"

He snorts. "No. But we do belong to darkness, to chaos. To violence. Long ago our elders decided to take control of what they were, to alter our place in the world for our own benefit. But as you saw last night in that apartment, we still affect the world of light. We still bring chaos even when we attempt to remain neutral. To try to be otherwise only brings pain. And not the good kind."

My chest tightens. I knew all of this on some level, but hearing it laid out like this hurts. I lost so much more than my heartbeat when that gun went off.

"What would happen if we tried? I mean, not *we*." I rub my hand over the solid reality of his upper arm to ground myself. "Not you and me. But what if a vampire tried to hold on to the light? Made friends, say with a human, if the vampires wouldn't..." I trail off.

Daniel clenches his teeth, tightening the muscles of his jaw. "That would unquestionably make that vampire a danger to her species. It would make her a security threat, and it would make a mockery of what we are. A vampire like that would be unsuited to her society, and she would no doubt find herself outcast."

I lick my lips, but my mouth has gone so dry from hearing that last word that it does me no good. No more clubs. No more approved feedings. There would be no choice but to go rogue, be hunted, and face death.

Or to go into true isolation, I suppose, living a nomadic life, feeding when possible, and hoping not to cause enough of a stir to threaten our secrecy and bring the hunters down. There's only one punishment for those who become a threat to our world.

I shudder. I might prefer execution over slow starvation if I didn't know there was nothing for us after. No hell. No heaven. No reincarnation. Nothing.

It does make following the rules and continuing an unlife of glorious feeding and fucking and star-filled night gazing rather appealing.

"I understand. I was just asking." It hurts. It's not like I expected to find a great romance after death, but the knowledge that I'll never truly find the deep, selfless affection I once craved cuts me deep.

"Just remember that you're here." His touch becomes more firm as it traces the curves of my body. "You've lost a lot, but the darkness gives more if we allow it. Strength. Speed. Perception. The glory of the night over the glare of the sun." He places a teasing kiss on my shoulder. "The miracle of our bodies obeying our commands with no heartbeat to sustain them. The void is not nothing. It is the mirror of what you once had, but deeper."

I frown at him. "Keep talking."

He smiles. "You've grazed the surface of it these past

few days, but there's so much more. Imagine that the void, the darkness you feel within you, is a vast ocean reflecting the stars. It's cold and mysterious in ways that the airy world above will never understand." His accent has grown thick. Unguarded. "There are dangers in the depths, and wonders. You're playing in the shallows now. I'm hardly any deeper. But I know there's more."

There's a light in his eyes as he speaks. Not the zealous glint of an evangelist, but something more like wonder.

"That is something," I agree. I don't add that I'd rather explore the depths with him than alone. "Why have you never told me this before?"

"Would you have understood before this past week?"

"No, I suppose not. And I guess Trixie already gets it, doesn't she?"

"I'm not sure."

I smile shyly at him. Daniel understands me on a deeper level than I ever realized. "You're not a bad teacher, you know. Even if you hate doing it."

"Good. Shall we get back to what I do enjoy, then?" His words are gentle and teasing, not harsh and selfish like he's supposed to be.

"I could probably be convinced."

He bares his teeth, then presses his lips to my sternum, my stomach. Trailing downward.

This is good. It isn't the existence I imagined at one time, but I can find meaning here. I know I can. The choice before me isn't light or darkness. It's darkness or nothing. And I don't want to be empty anymore.

Daniel's tongue ends my distraction, and I draw a sharp breath.

His phone rings.

"Shit." My voice, not his. He's already rolled off the bed to retrieve the phone from his pocket.

"Yes?" His vocal mask is back on. All business. "Of course. Right away." He closes the phone and gathers his clothes. "We'll resume this later, Aviva." Not a question. It's not like I would have declined, anyway.

"What's happening?"

"More bodies. Katya and Trixie are heading over there now." He hesitates. "It's up to you whether you want to come."

"What? Of course I want to."

"Very good."

"Why wouldn't I?"

He sits on the edge of the bed. "You'll need to watch yourself today," he says slowly, as though choosing his words carefully. "With Katya at the scene, you mustn't let on what you're thinking about the victims."

"Did I not hide it well last night?"

He reaches up to rub the back of his neck, and the moonlight picks out the faint lines on the front of his shoulder where I bit him last night. They're already healing. It's sort of a shame. They looked good on him.

"Everything I just said about how a vampire forming the wrong kinds of relationships can find herself in a difficult position goes double when an elder is around. Katya ranks just under Miranda. If she sees weakness, she will not hesitate to end it. That's good for someone like Trixie, whose natural inclinations make her easy to shape to our ideal."

"But I'm the runt of the litter, so I'd better prove myself before our mistress decides to drown me?"

His eyebrows rise in surprise. He seems pleased, and my good student side can't help feeling glad about that in spite of the threat he's describing. "Precisely. I wasn't concerned about Wallace the other night. Most younger and less-ambitious vampires will leave you be as long as you don't threaten them. They don't want to make enemies any more than you or I do. But Katya has been around long enough that her position is secure, and she doesn't have much compassion for anyone who threatens us. It's what makes her a great hunter." He huffs out a little laugh. "I thought I might pass out when she showed up at the suicide and I couldn't warn you. I was relieved when you handled things so well."

My stomach drops. What if I hadn't? What if, in opening myself to the shadows of the person who had died, I had betrayed my connection to that life? Surely she'd have listened to Daniel if he said I was making progress.

Or maybe he'd have been in trouble for allowing my

weakness to continue in the interest of allowing me to explore my strength.

Pain flashes through my temples. I'm clenching my jaw hard enough that I might have cracked softer teeth. I force myself to relax.

"I appreciate the warning. I can handle this." I stride past him to my dresser, searching for something that looks at least half as professional as Katya looked last night. "I won't try to open myself to the shadows this time," I assure him, making the decision as I speak. "They're interesting, but they haven't showed me anything that helps with the investigation." I slip into a sweater and dark pants, then swipe at the dark mascara that's smudged under my eyes. Smoky. Not bad. "I think you were right. All I needed was to let go of my struggle. I'll move forward now. See what the void brings me."

I still don't want to lose myself. Not yet. But maybe I can step a little deeper. A little further away from my attachments.

I glance at Daniel in the mirror. He nods, but he doesn't look nearly as confident as I'm trying to feel.

***

It's just past sunset when we leave the house. It's been raining all day, and the remaining sunlight is all but invisible behind thick cloud cover. We head for Mount Pearl and cut a loop back into St. John's, into a newer neighbourhood of pretty, multi-coloured houses that celebrate the local image of homes by the shore without the cost and weather conditions of actual waterfront property. Large family houses—they probably cost a nice sum when the housing boom was at its peak. They're nice, but very *neighbourhoody*, with new trucks in the driveways standing over toppled bicycles like watchful parents and cute Easter decorations still clinging to some of the windows. The whole area is terribly modern Leave It To Beaver with its cozy, winding streets and wide, welcoming porches.

Just a few years ago I'd have swooned over the idea of something like this in my future. Now all I can imagine is how I'd stick out as the local weirdo if I moved in around here. Our lair might not be fancy, but it does have the advantage of neighbours who mind their own business as long as we mind ours.

Daniel pulls up not far from the freshly paved driveway of a big house at the end of a cul-de-sac. The biggest house on the street, in fact. A flagship home for the new subdivision. White columns on the porch support a sloped, slate-grey roof that peeks out from under massive second-storey windows. Double garage. Generous yard.

Rich folks.

Trixie is waiting at the door, and she bounces down the steps to greet us. They haven't turned the porch lights on. "Hurry up!"

You'd think she was dragging us into a birthday party rather than a crime scene.

"What's the matter, Trixie?" Daniel asks. "Scared they're going to wake up before we get there?"

She gives him an appraising look. "That was almost a joke. Better watch yourself."

We hang back as she leads the way up to the elegant yet homey wooden door. "Better watch that, indeed," I say in a low voice, quiet enough that even Trixie won't overhear. "You're in a good mood, and Katya's a hell of a lot more observant than Trixie is."

Daniel rolls his shoulders back. "We didn't do anything wrong. Katya would think it strange if nothing had happened. But you're right. I'll try to keep my joie de Viva under wraps."

I cringe. "No. No jokes, no puns, and definitely no dad jokes. You're out of practice. Give it time."

The quick grin he flashes me makes me wish I'd just ignored him. I need to learn not to give anyone weapons to use against me.

"I mean, if turning me off is your intention," I continue, but don't have time to finish. We step into the silence of a foyer the size of a small conference room. Wasted space, really, but I suppose the people who lived here could afford to waste it. The floors are tiled in white marble, and the wide staircase to our left is a study in casual elegance. It sweeps up the curved wall, its shining wooden bannister completely ignored by Trixie as she leads the way up.

White carpet on the stairs. No children, then.

"Interesting scene this time," Trixie says as she waits for us to catch up. "Doesn't look like we're going to strike it lucky here, though."

I shouldn't feel disappointed by that. I don't know these rogues, but I know enough to expect them not to screw up in any obvious fashion.

"How was your day?" I ask Trixie.

"Oh, fine. Katya couldn't be there to meet me at the hotel, so I just got settled in and slept. You look tired."

I don't answer that.

Everything is light and airy until we approach the master bedroom at the end of the hall. Even if I had walked in here blind, I would have known what had happened. The air is thick and heavy. I open myself to it, testing my perceptions. No shadows, but I sense pain. Terror. It's objective, though. Distant. Not something I feel in myself.

Katya steps out of the room. She's dressed in a suit again, charcoal grey this time. She's pulled her striking hair back into an elegant bun at the back of her neck, and it makes her look as severe as Daniel's warning about her. I stand up straighter and promise myself again that I won't do anything stupid.

"It's the same crew as the others, if I've interpreted the

reports correctly," she says with a sigh, pulling clear latex gloves off her long fingers.

"Feeding for fun?" Daniel asks.

Katya nods toward the double doors to the master bedroom, only one of which stands open. "See for yourself. Looks like these victims did a better job of fighting back."

Daniel leads again, stepping slowly into the room, and I follow close behind.

At least they don't seem to have wasted as much blood this time.

More bungee cords. The man is naked, tied to a faux-antique chair that I assume was only supposed to be for decoration. It hardly looks like a comfortable place to relax. Or to die. He's slumped forward as far as the bonds will allow, jaw slack, eyes wide and staring down at his feet. The paired wounds on his neck stand out against his drained-pale skin, which still holds the echo of a deep tan. He's handsome, or would have been, once. His fresh, traditional haircut, as well as the dark suit hanging on a waist-high rack in the corner behind him, give him away as a professional of some sort.

Katya said it looked like they fought back. The man's face is beaten, his knuckles cracked where he hit someone or something. I bet the rogues enjoyed that.

I force myself to ignore the anguish in his staring eyes and turn to take in the rest of the scene.

A bed occupies the other half of the spacious room, a

king-sized affair in dark wood piled with white blankets that spill onto the floor in a heap. I can't see much with Daniel standing in the way. I move to look around him, and he places a hand on my arm.

Not holding me back. Warning me. He leans in, and his broad chest fills my vision. "Remember."

"I'll be fine."

He squeezes my upper arm and lets go.

I won't be fine.

I close my eyes, just for a moment. I have to be okay with this.

When I open them, Katya is watching. So is the technician who I so impressed at the first crime scene. Waiting.

My stomach turns and my heart seems to drop down into it, but I force my expression to remain hard and neutral as I take in the scene.

More bungee cords, this time tying a young woman to the bedposts, spread out in an x-shape. Naked as her husband. Her neck bears the marks of feeding, as well, but whoever took her didn't get all of her blood. They kept it off the white carpet and the walls, but a horrifying amount has soaked into the sheets and the mattress beneath her, with the rest of it smeared over her hips, her thighs, and her belly. She's been slashed with a knife like the last one, and elongated burn marks spot her arms, chest, and the few places on her legs I can see through the blood. A curling iron rests on the bedside table.

Cordless. How convenient for them.

Bile rises in my throat, and I force it back. At least we didn't have a chance to stop for coffee this time.

The victim's face looks incongruously peaceful. I suppose death was a mercy for her.

"When did this happen?" I ask Katya. My voice is steady. Good. But the cold tone of it shocks me.

This is who I'm supposed to be. How horrible.

"Early this morning," Wallace answers for her. I hadn't noticed him in the corner, examining the brushes on the bottom of a fancy vacuum cleaner. Katya's bodyguard Christopher stands next to him, arms crossed, scowling.

I look back at the woman on the bed and can't help comparing her morning with mine.

I force myself to look away. I didn't do this. If I'm going to feel guilty about enjoying myself in my bed while she died in hers, it can happen later.

I look back to the man. I don't want to imagine what he saw as he died. Can't let myself go there.

I'd like to open a window to let the fresh air blow away some of the heaviness in here, but they'll want to keep the scene closed. I can look out, though. I hope it will look like I'm considering angles of approach. Even if it doesn't, it has to look better than me puking in the full ensuite or racing headlong down the stairs and out the front door.

Filthy snow in hard, melted drifts dots the dark lawns of neighbours who have no idea what's happened here. It's

Friday. Surely he missed work today, and I assume she did, too. A planned long weekend, maybe. Taking some time off together. Whatever the reason, no one seems to think it's odd that these two have disappeared.

The houses on the street are all nice, but not one is as impressive as this one. I wonder if the neighbours envied these people and rolled their eyes at the Escalade in the driveway. Or maybe the victims were the kind of people you sort of hate for their perfect life, but they chat with you over the back fence and give out full-size chocolate bars at Halloween, offer cuttings from their best garden plants and always remember to bring over a little something to welcome the new family on the street, so you can't really hate them.

Shadows swirl behind me, felt more than seen, as I close my eyes and rest my forehead against the cool glass. Vague shapes that won't tell me anything I don't know. They might make this worse for me, though. I'm not interested.

I look to Daniel. He's watching me, understanding that I'm struggling. It's written in his eyes and the mask-still expression that threatens to give me away even if I don't do it myself. I give him a little smile.

I'm fine, really.

Daniel turns back to the technician, who's telling him something about a small stain on the carpet. A footprint, if we're lucky, but I'm guessing we won't be.

I close the curtains tight as Katya turns on a bedside lamp. The dim light illuminates a new aspect to the scene, something darker, more like it might have looked less than twenty-four hours ago when these people died. Nothing helpful jumps out, though.

Same rogues, same craving for terror and pain, same careful clean-up.

Katya prowls around the room. Gracefully, like a dancer. I let my eyes follow her without really thinking about it, trying instead to focus on a creeping sense that something is wrong. I can't place why, though. It's not the shadows. More like a sense of familiarity.

Katya steps nimbly around the man in the chair, and a sense of déjà vu sweeps over me. I close my eyes, and the shadows swirl. A faint female voice begs for mercy.

I need to look at something else. Something to clear my head. I was wrong. I obviously can't handle this. I try telling myself that the shadows are something like the afterglow that used to hide behind my eyelids if I looked at the sun, but it doesn't help.

I don't know how everyone else is ignoring the choking heaviness in the air.

Maybe Daniel was right to want to leave me behind. He'll never admit he was wrong about me, but there's a chance I'm not cut out for this work. Maybe I am destined to be powerful, but none of the skills I'm developing now are helping here.

Human relations, maybe, if I can separate myself from my compassion and prove myself trustworthy. Something where my connection to them can help without turning my stomach.

The feeling comes again. Voices. Shadows.

Fuck it. There's something here, begging me to see it. I take a deep breath, slowly and quietly so no one will notice and think me odd. I hold it, ordering my mind to calm itself. The shadows continue to swirl, sensed rather than seen now that my eyes are open.

Fine. I can do this. I can investigate in my own way without freaking out. If I give into it for a minute, let myself think about them and the tragedy of their deaths, I'll see the shadows more clearly. I'll prove to myself that there's nothing more I can do for these people, and maybe I can get rid of that horrible creeping sense that something is descending on all of us.

A framed photo catches my eye. Two people, barely recognizable as the tormented bodies we're all slowly becoming well acquainted with. She in a long strapless wedding dress, him looking very tall, dark, and handsome in his black tux. They had their photos done by the ocean, and her veil blows in the wind. No rigidly posed portrait here. They're laughing, and he's going in for a kiss as she wrinkles her nose and swats at him with her bright pink bouquet. Maybe she didn't want to smudge her perfect lipstick. Maybe they were just playful like that.

I bet they were happy. I bet they expected to grow old together.

The feeling of terrible wrongness comes again as the idea of their lost future tugs hard at my heart. It's like a ghost in the room, watching me. I spin around, but nothing has changed. Katya stands over the woman's body, explaining something to Trixie, who's eating up every syllable that falls from the elder's lips.

Trixie turns away, and Katya's expression changes, just for an instant. She looks at the body almost affectionately, and a smile twitches at one corner of her mouth.

Not like an investigator or a hunter, but like an artist looking over her work.

No.

I squeeze my eyes closed and turn slowly away, not caring whether anyone notices. The shadows encroach again, clearer and sharper than they were when I tried to fight them away. And there it is. The graceful glide of a slim shadow, trailing long hair behind it. No details, but the silhouette is—

No. Still no. Katya is an elder. Respected by everyone from Trixie to Daniel to Miranda herself. And if she did have exotic tastes, she could get anything she wanted at the club. I'm sure she would have full access to the dark vials on Miranda's wall if nothing available at the bar pleased her. She has no reason to go rogue. She hunts them, for fuck's sake. She's one of ours, one of the best.

I'm wrong. That's all. And if Katya got so much as a whiff of what I'm thinking right now, she would have my ass shipped off to Nunavut.

It's just a feeling. I let myself feel too much. I see the victims as people rather than clues, and I'm misleading myself. Maybe it's because I'm wary of her after what Daniel told me about her, and my subconscious is... Shit, I wish I'd studied psychology so I knew what the hell was happening in the depths of my mind right now. The void within me wouldn't have seen any of this and been misled as my emotions have. I'm trusting the wrong part of myself, and Daniel was right. It's bad. It could get me killed.

I open my eyes and turn to get back to work, ignoring the return of that déjà vu sensation as Katya moves around the room.

She obviously feels me watching her. She turns and smiles.

I don't know her well enough to know whether the coldness in her eyes is directed at me, or if that's just the way she is. But when I reach deep and draw on the power of the darkness that's in me, I feel it. Malice radiating off of her as she turns back to the body, looking as cold and analytical as can be.

Maybe her ill-will is toward the rogues.

Or maybe I'm in deeper trouble than I've been in since the night I died.

CHAPTER THIRTEEN

F uck.

I was hoping that sleeping for a day would make things clearer for me, maybe give me time to put things in perspective. I haven't dreamed since my last night alive, but sleep usually does help with these things. I should have known I wouldn't be so lucky this time. I've wakened to a brand new night with zero insights and no less confusion than I came to bed with.

We didn't get home until almost dawn, and Daniel and I dragged ourselves to our separate beds without a word of discussion on the matter. Nothing is assumed in our situation. We're not here to hang out, to snuggle in bed as we drift off to sleep, to share our feelings about the night. He asked on the ride home if I wanted to talk about anything that had happened, and *not yet* was all I had to offer.

I had too many thoughts, and too many of them

heading in opposite directions. I wanted to approach Daniel with a clear head and a solid idea of what might be going on, not with flighty thoughts and vague feelings that seem to come from a place within me that's taboo in our world.

Problem is, I've still got nothing.

I get up to open the curtains, letting the light from the streetlamp outside illuminate the room as I pace between the bed and the dresser. It's not a pleasant light, but I need something. If I sit in the dark I'll drift too far.

And I do feel like I'm drifting.

I've come so far since Daniel told me to just let myself be what I am. My senses are improved, and my extrasensory perceptions have soared. I'm getting faster, stronger, experiencing clarity in my training... all good and proper things that come from the void within me.

But then there's this other thing. The way I seem to be connected with the victims of these horrific crimes. What the hell is that? I don't think I'm seeing ghosts. I want to believe that there's something for people like them after death, that they're not hanging around here with the likes of us, still suffering. But I'm clearly sensing something, and impressions left by their trauma seems like the only reasonable explanation.

I can't help but notice that my definition of "reasonable" has expanded exponentially since my death.

All I know for sure is that I saw something. I caught a

glimpse of it at the first murder scene, and didn't care to look closer. Who would, when it feels like you're going insane? There was less of it at the suicide, even when I tried to open myself. But this time...

This time, I felt like it was real. I know what I saw, what I felt. The problem is, I don't know whether I can trust my perceptions.

I don't feel crazy at all. I really think these emotions and images are coming from outside of me.

But I don't want to be right. And I don't want to think about what Daniel would say if he knew what I'm thinking about Katya. Every time I remember her pleased little smile and the ill-will that radiated from her, I get chills.

I flop back on the bed and pull a pillow over my eyes, blocking out the light. Maybe drifting isn't such a bad idea.

"Aviva?"

I don't answer. Daniel steps into the room.

"What happened last night?"

I toss my pillow to the floor and sit up. "Are you asking as a friend, my trainer, or the guy who's fucking me and feels like he should ask?"

He sits beside me. "I'm no longer the second, and the third is irrelevant. At least, it shouldn't make any difference to this discussion."

He really sounds like he means that. This will take a lot of getting used to.

"So," he says slowly, "we could say it's the first, though

that's tricky as well. How about a concerned colleague and mentor who's fucking you and feels like he should ask?"

I laugh in spite of the heaviness in my chest that's threatening to make me one with the bed again. It cuts off sharply as I consider what I'm about to tell him.

And I am. All of it. Wasn't I thinking not long ago that he seems to understand me? He won't judge me as quickly or as harshly as he says Katya would. He'll listen. He'll tell me what he knows about this shit.

And so I tell him everything I experienced at that big, beautiful house.

He goes paler than he usually is when I mention Katya looking at the body, but I press on and explain about the shadow.

Her shadow.

His brow furrows, and he doesn't say anything for a minute—one that feels like it's stretching into hours. Finally he says, "This is concerning."

I relax. "Thank you."

He turns slowly to me. "It was a mistake for me to tell you to stop trying to let go of your humanity."

If I had a heartbeat, it would have fallen still at the regret in his voice. "What do you mean?"

"It's obviously causing you more problems than I had anticipated. I've been so pleased with your progress, but it's not worth this cost."

Cold prickles creep over my arms and back. "You don't believe me?"

He leans forward, resting his elbows on his knees. "I believe that you're telling me the truth about what you saw and felt."

"But?"

He glances at the window, then back to me, locking his gaze to mine. "Aviva, think about what you're saying. Who you're accusing of unthinkable crimes. Katya is an elder, but it goes deeper than that. She has been instrumental in the development of our social structure—a key element in negotiating relations with vampires around the world. She knows better than any of us, except maybe Miranda and the other elders, what we stand to lose. Katya helped design the system that makes stock available to us. She was there when they made the laws about killing, and every squad of rogue hunters on this continent answers to her." He shakes his head. "There's no one further above suspicion."

I swallow back the lump of disappointment in my throat. What did I expect? It does sound crazy. Even I'm doubting myself. And Daniel has always made it perfectly clear that our loyalty is to Maelstrom, our elders, and finally, ourselves. Not to each other. Not to new vampires who have no idea how to control their perceptions.

He's not my boyfriend. There's no blind loyalty here. And maybe that's for the best, if I'm wrong.

"And the malice I felt from her?"

"You can't assume it was directed at you. It's only natural she would feel it toward the rogues when she looked at the body. I'd be more surprised if she didn't."

We're silent for a minute. "What if I was right?" I ask, barely whispering.

He presses his lips into a tight line as he considers that. "You'd be in more danger than she would if you accused her."

He says it so matter-of-factly that I can't even be surprised. Of course I would be. I'm nothing. She's an elder.

An elder who would never kill, never mind so openly. I'm wrong. I have to be.

I press the heels of my hands to my eyes, trying to shove my swirling thoughts into some kind of order. It doesn't help.

"So what do I do with what I saw? How do I make sense of that?"

His phone rings, filling the room with its electronic noise. He reaches slowly for his pocket, obviously dreading the call as much as I am.

I don't want to hear that anyone else has died.

"Yes?" He's silent, listening, tensed like he's about to fight someone. He stands, but doesn't move toward the door. "Very good. I'll see you there. No, not this time."

He hangs up. "I have to go."

My stomach clenches, but I rise from the bed. "Where are we going?"

"Not you, Aviva. Take tonight off. Give yourself some time to think."

He hasn't touched me, but he might as well have pushed me down. I sit again, glaring up at him. It's not that I want to go. Why would I want to see what they've done, or be faced with the darker potential of what I am? But I can help. If I'm wrong about Katya, so be it, but I want to help. I hadn't realized how much until just now, when Daniel told me I couldn't.

When did I become this contrary?

Daniel crouches in front of me and places a hand on my thigh. I resist the urge to pull away. "Listen to me, please."

Daniel doesn't say please. Daniel gives orders. It's enough to stop any tirade I'd be tempted to go off on. He holds my gaze, and I couldn't look away even if I wanted to.

"I don't know what's happening with you. We'll figure it out. I don't doubt that you're coming into your powers now, or that they might help us here. But you are young and untested, and I think you need practice in interpreting what you're seeing and feeling." His fingers tighten on my leg. "I want your help. But Katya will be there today, and based on what I saw from you at the last scene, I don't think it's a good idea for you to be around her."

"You don't trust me?"

"I don't want to see you in trouble. Katya is not someone you want to make an enemy of. She doesn't care whether you like her, but if she thinks you are questioning her authority or undermining her in any way, she will turn everyone against you. She is not merciful. She will not tolerate your suspicions if she catches on. Please. Stay away from her until we figure this out. For my sake."

I grit my teeth. I get it. I do. At least he's not giving orders now. But I hate *for your own good* arguments. Always have. They make me feel like a child. And even though Daniel knows Katya far better than I do, even though he's probably seen vampires face her ire, and even though I like that he cares enough to protect me—which he shouldn't, if he respects himself as a proper vampire—it rankles me.

I don't say anything, and he gets up to leave.

"It's not just Katya," he adds. "If any elder doubts your loyalty to them or to Maelstrom, you'll be turned out."

My blood chills as I imagine having to go rogue, Daniel hunting me like a common criminal.

"Even if I'm right about her?"

He looks out the window. "Even if you are, which you are not, and I suggest you practice letting go of the idea... Even then, my advice to you would be to let it go. You would not win this battle, and there's no reason for you to take it on."

"Not even if my silence means more people will die?"

"That's not your concern. Or mine. We're handling the potential consequences of the crime scenes. We won't be exposed."

Heat rises in me at his icy tone. "Shit, Daniel. How does this not matter to you? Those children, that couple. Were you this fucking cold when you were alive, or was it just that easy for you to let it all go when you died?"

His lip curls in rage, and he hits me with a glare that ices over all the anger that was building in my blood. "I was too compassionate when I was alive, too willing to sacrifice myself, and it cost me things I won't think or speak of now. I experienced hell in its truest form before my death. Letting go of my humanity afterward was the only way I managed to stay sane. I'd advise you to do the same if you value your future."

He stalks out of the room and slams the door behind him.

I lie down and pull the pillow back over my head.

Fuck.

God, these shows are stupid.

I'm not really supposed to be watching this shit. And I'm not, technically. I'm listening to the TV like it was a radio play, since I can't be bothered to dig out the glasses that would protect my eyes from the irritating flashes of the screen.

We're not even encouraged to listen to the news, let alone dramas about teenage vampires and their ridiculous romantic entanglements, and I'm not so far gone that I need to work hard at keeping up with modern culture. That's not to say programs like this don't have their uses, though. When the living watch and read this fake vampire stuff, it blinds them to the reality that lurks so close to the surface of their ignorant, shallow world. It's another layer of protection for us, as is the fact that the living like to play-act at being vampires. It would all be insulting if it wasn't so effective at making people disbelieve in the real thing.

I'm not really paying attention to the on-screen melo-drama, but it's good to have the noise in the background. I can tune it out while I think.

And I have been thinking. Daniel's been gone for twelve hours, and I haven't yet taken a break from sorting through the situation I've got myself into.

Twelve hours. I hope that means they found some-thing. He hasn't tried to reach me to let me know.

I still have no idea whether I'm wrong about Katya. That's not something I can answer without more informa-tion, so I've set it aside. That question is just masking the bigger one.

The one about who and what I am.

Until last week, I was a fuck-up. Worthy of being

called a vampire, certainly, but not able to connect with my deeper nature, even if I hid that fact well. I've found the key to that. But the key is my compassion for the living, and the gift it has unlocked is something I can only call empathy. I'm sensing the emotions imprinted on the places where people died, catching glimpses of the experience through their eyes.

I've never heard of this. It's not strange for a vampire to have unique gifts, of course—Miranda's perception of thoughts is certainly not typical, and Daniel can mask himself better than anyone else I know. I'm not a freak or a superhero for having a talent, but it is a strange one for a creature that's supposed to be cut off from the human world.

I shouldn't have a gift that makes me feel like I have scraps of a soul clinging to me.

Maybe this is why I was ill-suited to become a vampire. Even now, after I've found a gift and some level of acceptance for my situation, I'm not like the others. Not like Trixie, or even Daniel.

I've seen my difference as a weakness. Everyone has, starting at the facility where I woke after my transformation. My lingering connection to life has held me back, but it's turned out to be the key to my gifts.

Why?

I'm not supposed to think about *why*. Why is a question for the living. I belong to the void now, to chaos. There is no why. There is only what is, what we choose and what we do.

But what if I still have a purpose?

Or better yet, what if I can still choose one for myself?

The thought quickens something in me. I am what I am. Maybe there's no greater reason for that, but I can choose to do good with my gift. I'm the only one willing to protect the living for their own sake, rather than to keep our world secret. And yes, my desire to do that is wrong, according to vampires. But I don't care that it's wrong. I have to help them. I have to find the answers, and there's a chance that my weird, intensely wrong gift is what could catch the rogues, assuming I sort that gift out from my mess of personal issues.

I'm not going to let Katya, my own mixed-up mind, or my inexperience get in the way of that. Daniel can't argue with me there. Getting rid of these rogues will be good for all of us. He believed I'd make a good hunter, and for the first time, I think maybe he wasn't wrong.

I sink back into the deep couch cushions. I feel good about this. If I let go of my suspicions about Katya—which logically make no sense, I see that now—I can do great things. Maybe keep working with Daniel.

That wouldn't be terrible, assuming he still wants me. I think I hurt him earlier. I didn't know that was possible. Daniel's an emotional tank. He might get irritated by disrespect or act angry if his subordinates aren't doing their best, but he's always seemed untouchable on any deep level. I don't know why me accusing him of exactly what he should be proud of made him turn on me, but I am sorry.

I like him. Not just because he's nice to look at, not just because his excessive self-control and competence are kind of sexy, and not just because I respect him. He's actually pretty cool when he lets his guard down. He's a fucking beast in bed, and resting next to him was amazing. He's always wanted what was best for me, even if his ways of getting me there haven't exactly been what my living self would have looked for in a friend or a lover.

I can't want him as either. He's not offering those things, and I shouldn't expect them. But I don't want to push him away. I don't know exactly what I'll be apologizing for, but I should—

The lock thunks, and the front door swings open with a slight creak. I jump up, turn off the TV, and prowl slowly toward the front hall.

Daniel takes off the flat cap he's got pulled low over his eyes to protect himself from the sun that's just risen behind heavy clouds, then heads to the kitchen to splash cold water on his face and ears. He's not looking burned, but he can't be comfortable right now. I give him a minute to dry off and relax in the curtained darkness of the house before I speak.

"I want to go to the scene. If you want me to avoid Katya, that's fine, though I think it will be okay."

He turns to me, but doesn't say anything.

"See, I really think I can help," I continue. "And I don't know whether I can do that if I let go of who I am, or my connections to the living… I don't even know whether those are separate things. Maybe I'm just broken or wrong, and maybe I shouldn't have been made at all, but I'm here. And I feel like I can help. And I'm sorry for whatever I said that pissed you off."

He crosses the kitchen in three long strides and pulls me close, burying his nose in my hair and inhaling deeply as his arms tighten around me.

"I hated myself for leaving like that," he says quietly. "I shouldn't have lost my temper."

That's it. No explanation of what he meant or why whatever memory I sparked hurt him. I'd be upset by that if I didn't think that what he's offering me now is more than he can afford if he wants to maintain the proper distance between us.

This isn't a television show. Neither of us can offer impassioned pleas for forgiveness or promises to do better. We're not those creatures, and there's no point in wanting what I can't have.

This, though, I can enjoy. His arms around me. Feeling like we're maybe getting back toward being on the same team. Forgiveness, which I suspect is not high on the list of vampire virtues.

I turn my face toward him, brushing my lips across his

brow. Not a kiss. Not when sex shouldn't be on the menu. But I can't help craving the feel of his skin on mine. On a whim, I reach deep into the void within me and try to feel him. I consider him as a man, as a vampire, rather than as my trainer and elder. Someone whose emotions might run as deep and true as mine, but who's too damn good at hiding them.

It's faint, but I catch something. Relief. Comfort filling him now that he's home with me and away from the light and the violence outside our door. Something in my chest slips a notch, and I feel myself expanding. Understanding. Caring more than I should.

He releases me, and I reluctantly let my arms fall to my sides.

"I'll take you back tonight," he says. "I've been giving it a lot of thought, and I'd like to see what you make of things. The bodies are gone now, but it would be interesting to see what you can do with the empty house before humans come poking around. Any insights would be helpful at this point, and if you feel up for it..." He shrugs. "I don't want to stop you, Aviva. If this is your gift, and if it's as powerful as I've always suspected you might be, I want to see you master it. But I don't want it to cost you more than it's worth. I may have done a poor job of making that clear earlier."

I smile. "There's a good chance I just didn't want to hear it."

He's willing to help me. That's more than I have any right to expect, given what I'm dealing with right now and the danger I'm becoming to myself.

I don't know how far I can trust him to follow me, but this is a start.

CHAPTER FOURTEEN

We spend the day in our own beds and hit the road first thing, driving through the thin post-sunset light toward Mount Pearl. The smaller town blends in with St. John's. I wouldn't know where one ended and the other began if not for the tourist-friendly sign thanking me for visiting the city I now call home. Daniel fills me in as he drives.

"We're going to have trouble keeping this one quiet," he says. His voice is even, but too tight for me to think he's really as calm as he's pretending to be. "They're not just getting bolder with their timing and leaving the murders staged for us to find. They're choosing victims who will be missed now, and quickly."

I rest my head against the window beside me. "Who was it?"

He doesn't answer, but to be fair, he's in the middle of

navigating heavy traffic and washed-out lane markings. I let the question drop. I'll find out soon enough.

It doesn't make sense. Rogues are supposed to be vampires on the run. If it were me on the loose, desperate for a meal, I'd be taking victims quietly, trying not to bring the hunters down on me. Of course, in my case, I'd rather die than kill. But if I had to do it, I certainly wouldn't be leaving my messes for others to clean up.

"Was there any evidence this time?"

He shakes his head. "Nothing useful. What we thought was vampire blood turned out to be watered-down human."

"So they're just fucking with us now."

His lips tighten. "Basically."

"This goes beyond hunger or exotic tastes, doesn't it?"

"We think so."

He's not offering me much. He seems dull, like he needs to feed, and I don't feel much better. That's the plan as soon as we're done here—head to the club, replenish, regroup. I wish we'd gone there first, but Daniel wanted to get me out here before the living descend on the scene. It's too early to find good stock at the club, anyway.

I almost wish Daniel had come to bed with me today. As it turns out, the pleasure of his touch makes me feel almost as alive as feeding does. I couldn't give up blood in favour of fucking, but it would be fun to try.

I glance down at his hand gripping the gear shift, the

exposed forearm where his shirt sleeve is rolled up, smooth muscle under pale skin.

Like I needed another addiction. I look away.

The house is a nice two-storey with a wide driveway, white siding, and a huge front window looking out onto a yard with high hedges that shield the house from the street. Daniel pulls past a junky-looking green Jetta and parks around back, where we're invisible to anyone not on the property.

Daniel opens the back door and sticks his head into the house, listening for a moment before he stands aside and lets me lead the way in. "I don't know whether them taking the bodies away will affect you."

"We'll see."

The door opens into a tiny laundry room strewn with expensive, beat-up sneakers and a mess of coats tossed on top of the front-loading washer. I pick my way through the minefield and into the kitchen. I'd peg the house at around thirty years old, but the kitchen is much newer, renovated in that fake-shabby country style with distressed white cabinets and a tall copper faucet over a farmhouse-style sink. It costs a lot to look this pleasantly run-down, but whoever was here last didn't show a lot of respect for that obvious fact. The dark wood countertops are covered in uncapped soda bottles and an array of cheap booze, and a torn-open bag of ice has melted onto the floor. Bowls of party mix and chips sit half-empty on the big wooden table in the dining room that's visible through an open glass door.

I open the brushed steel fridge. Glass containers labelled with contents and cooking instructions look to hold about a week's worth of prepared meals.

"Someone's parents went away?" Not that I need to ask.

"Looks that way."

As soon as I step into the hallway that leads toward the front door, I catch the faint smell of blood. The sharp stink of the alcohol in the kitchen and cleaning products wafting up from the basement would be enough to mask it if we were limited to living senses, but we're not that lucky. Daniel and I are monsters. Even spoiled, dead blood calls to us.

I move toward the basement door without hesitation or direction from Daniel, and he follows a few steps behind. I suddenly realize that this is why he didn't give me details earlier. He wants me to take the lead and show him what I can do. It's a test as much as an opportunity.

I'm not sure whether I should be pissed about that. Maybe later. For now, I have a job to do.

A carpeted stairway leads to a finished basement. Death chokes the air down here, like its heaviness dragged it all underground. The space is divided into a large rec room and a few smaller rooms off a short hallway. Probably a furnace room, maybe a bathroom. It all has the newish air of the kitchen. The paint is fresh, but the dark brown carpet looks cheaper than anything they used to finish the kitchen. This was family space, not for company. Maybe not for parents.

Couches upholstered in worn brown leather face a big TV in the corner, and the coffee table that's been pushed to one side is covered in paper plates and pizza.

So much for those healthy, home-cooked meals in the fridge.

There's a diluted bloodstain surrounding a wooden chair in the corner, but I'm not going to start there. It can wait until I get a sense of things. I'm probably lucky our clean-up crew didn't tear up the carpet entirely. I don't imagine we leave much for the living to go on if it gets to the point of an investigation, though I notice they left any mess not directly related to the murder untouched. It's like the bodies were just plucked out of whatever life was happening before the rogues showed up.

In the open space in the centre of the room lies an empty wine bottle. Our investigation should be over, but I accept the gloves Daniel offers and slip them on before I pick it up. No point sending the police on a snipe hunt when they come and check for prints.

"Spin the bottle?"

Daniel shrugs. "We thought so. I didn't know kids did that anymore."

"I didn't, either. You'd think there would be an app or

something." High-schoolers, then. Old enough that some-one's parents left them and they decided to have a few friends over. Or they could have been college kids being goofy, but I'd like to think that anyone who can legally drink would have better taste than what's indicated by the open bar in the kitchen.

I close my eyes and try to focus. There's not a lot to go on here. I feel like I have an idea of who was here, but it doesn't go deeper than a logical analysis of the situation. I reach for the source of my power. The darkness fills me, soothing and beau-tiful as the night that's descending somewhere outside of this windowless basement, but it's not doing anything to help me.

No shadows. No emotion.

I open my eyes again. "How many bodies?"

"Eight."

I don't know what to say to that. It makes no sense. "The rogues just fed. There's no way they needed to hunt again. Do you think there are more of them than you suspected, or is this a statement?"

Daniel sinks onto one of the couches. "Both, maybe. This isn't the first time that we've seen something like this."

"Is that what Wallace mentioned back in Kilbride?" I didn't think much of it at the time. Just one more detail.

Daniel leans forward and rests his elbows on his knees, letting his hands dangle. "They dealt with something like this out in BC back in the autumn. Not nearly as visible, not apparently baiting us, but the same modus operandi. Torture. Multiple victims."

"And the rogues weren't caught?"

"No. They disappeared."

My shoulders tense. "Is that what we're supposed to hope for here?"

"If we don't catch them, it wouldn't be the worst thing."

I release the breath I didn't mean to draw. Of course that's what we want. Who cares if more people will die, as long as they do it somewhere else?

I can't let that happen. Not if it's in my power to stop it.

I'm about to return to my attempt to sense something when I pause and turn back to Daniel. "Was Katya there in BC? Just curious."

"She was called out to investigate, just as she was in this case."

Right. She was in London when all of this started here. I need to let go of that and focus on what I can get from this house. Maybe Daniel withholding information is actually a good thing. I'll get to see how much of what I get, if anything, is real.

Okay, eight kids. Small party, drinking a little, maybe a lot. Playing party games that seem innocent but could have ended in the kind of trouble that gets good girls kicked out

of their social circles while their boyfriends seek forgiveness and—

No. This isn't about me. Focus.

But that little remembrance of a life I'm supposed to
have left behind cracks something, and my gift awakens. I
can imagine them now, and even if I'm probably project-
ing, I'll go with it. See if I can open this window a little
more.

I'd guess, based on my own experiences, that they were
watching something on that TV at some point. Something
funny, I think.

Five girls. Three guys. I don't know where that comes
from, but I grab onto it. This isn't like the shadows or the
screaming emotion I got with bodies present, but it's
something.

I move closer to the TV. A copy of Monty Python's
Life of Brian rests on top of the DVD player. These kids
were into some retro shit, not unlike my own friends
once were.

If I'm right about the movie, I'm right about the other
stuff.

I move toward the chair in the corner. What a
fucking mess this must have been before we tidied up.
The dark carpet is stained rust in a blob that extends out
from the chair's wiped-down legs. I squint a little, and it
disappears. Human eyes wouldn't even notice. Traces of
blood don't call to them, after all. The paint on the wall is

shiny in patches. There was blood there, too, I have no doubt.

"Think this was an accident?" I ask.

"Maybe. Seems wasteful, but as you pointed out, they probably didn't really need to feed."

Blood is life. Someone's life spilled all over this floor, and for what? I can't wrap my mind around wanting to hurt someone like that. Since the suicide, I've felt more guilt over what we do at the club than I ever have before, but there's still a world of difference between that and this. What would compel a vampire to do this, to watch these kids long enough to know that no parent was coming home, planning the attack for a time when they were all in the basement and unable to escape their torture?

"I'm not getting anything." It's still all mental for me. I have that sense of who might have been here, but I almost don't want to ask in case I'm wrong.

Daniel stands and moves closer to me. "What were you doing at the last place when you saw what you did? When you had your suspicions, when you said you felt the fear and the pain?"

I wonder whether he has any idea how grateful I am that he thinks I'm not crazy.

"I was thinking about the people. Who they were when they were alive."

Daniel leans one shoulder against the wall and crosses his arms, inviting me to ignore him and get on with it. He must be even hungrier than I am, but for all he's rushing me he could have all the time in the world to wait.

I need to try something new. I've never touched the bodies or their belongings save for the first time, when I laid out freshly laundered blankets. Never tried to put myself where they were.

I don't want to, but I strip the gloves from my hands and step toward the chair, crouch, and rest one hand on the bloodstain.

The wave of terror and agony that hits me almost knocks me back on my ass. I grip the edge of the chair hard to keep my balance and ignore the tears that stream down my cheeks. There. The shadows. Faint, like the memory is paler without the body here, but the blood remembers. Dark shapes. Five of them. Laughter fills my ears, deep voices and higher ones, underscored by muffled female screams and shouting from down the hall. I squeeze my closed eyes tighter, and the shadows come into focus. No colour, but I catch a vague hint of bright eyes peering out of ski masks. That's all washed away by indistinct pain that fades as I grow cold.

I rise and walk to a more comfortable chair by the TV. No pain here, but the fear chokes me. It feels like there's something wrapped tight around my ribs, squeezing. I open my eyes and it disappears, along with the over-whelming emotions.

"They made one of them sit here while they did something to her friend over there." I gesture back to the other chair. "I don't know what." There are no visuals here, where there's no blood. Just emotion. Fear that screams like insanity. Disgust. Horror. But I don't know why she felt that way.

"The party was mostly girls, right?" I ask.

"Yes."

"Her friend died first. Then her. And..." I close my eyes again and let my other senses guide me down the hallway to a closed door. When I open it, panic washes over me. "And they brought the others out and fed on them when they were mad with fear. They'd left them trapped in here, listening to the screams in the other room. Like animals in a slaughterhouse."

I don't know how I know, but there's truth in my words. Everything I'm getting now is emotion.

"Three guys," I say aloud, certain now. "Five girls. Teenagers."

"Correct." Daniel has followed me, creeping like a cat, power and presence masked so he doesn't distract me. "And based on what we saw of the bodies, I'd say you're right in your assessment. See anything else?"

"The rogues wore masks."

"Interesting."

I look around the room. It's nearly empty, save for the hot water heater in the corner. No blood in here.

I should be pleased with getting so much. There's a lot

I'm not seeing, but I feel more open than I did before. I know now that physical connection opens me, as does letting myself think of the victims as people instead of bodies. But there's so much more, and I wish I'd come to see the bodies here, even if it meant facing Katya. What I'm getting now is nothing compared to what I felt last time, when I was absolutely certain of what I saw and felt.

When I was wrong.

My chest tightens again. How can I trust this gift when it steers me wrong? Maybe I wasn't open enough then. Or was freaked out by the bodies and misinterpreting cues. I'll do better now. Every crime scene I visit helps me learn control. But I think I've learned all I can here.

I lean into Daniel, and he rests his arms around me. Not restricting me, but supporting as I regroup. I'm suddenly exhausted, and I appreciate his presence. The intense focus I've been feeling is fading, along with the emotions. I'm weak, and hungry enough now that I feel woozy. My dark power quiets.

Daniel twists his fingers in the back of my hair, pulling gently downward, and I look up at him. "Anything else?"

"No. I'm done. I'm sorry I didn't get anything you didn't know."

He brushes his thumb across my cheekbone, wiping away the residue of the tears I'd already forgotten about.

"We did learn something, though," he says. "About you. I can tell you that nothing you pick up at scenes will be accepted as evidence. Ever. No matter how you prove yourself at times like this." He sounds regretful. "Empathy might as well be a sin for a vampire, if we had such a thing. It's an aspect of light, and not trustworthy."

"I remember. I'm not sorry about it, though."

"Nor am I." He holds my gaze again. God, his eyes are hypnotic. "Your gift is powerful, and highly suspect. I'd suggest keeping it between us, at least for now. But you can use it. Take what you learn with it, find real evidence and answers, use it in the moment on hunts and never feel that you have to explain your intuitions. You don't owe answers to anyone." He smiles again, warm and wide. "I'm proud of you. You're going to go far."

"Will you come with me?"

His smile falters. "As long as you need me, I suppose."

The moment is gone. His hand falls from my cheek, and he leads the way up the stairs.

I knew it was too much as soon as I said it.

We look through the rest of the house, but I'm either too tired or too disengaged to learn anything from what I see. The killings didn't happen up here, and knowing more about the victims doesn't help me. I almost trip over a stray Converse high top on the way out the door, and am too exhausted to wonder who it might have belonged to.

The sun has set, and a glorious, clear nighttime greets us.

As does a dark form leaning against Daniel's car.

Daniel and I freeze at the same moment as we step out onto the low back deck.

Daniel clears his throat. "Christopher."

I grit my teeth. Katya's goon. She may not be guilty, but she sure has a way of showing up everywhere I don't need to see her.

He pushes off from the car and takes one long step toward us, bald head shining in the moonlight.

"Fine evening for a continuing investigation," he observes.

"It is. Can we help you?" Daniel's tone gives nothing away.

"Just checking up on something for Katya. Think I got what I wanted, but I thought I'd wait to say hello."

"Very good." Daniel doesn't move, and neither do I. As far as I know, we have as much of a right to be here as anyone. Christopher might be irritating, but he's not going to hurt us.

He stretches his beefy arms out in front of him, cracking his knuckles, and walks down the driveway without another word. A moment later a car starts down the street, far enough away that we couldn't have heard its approach from inside the house.

Daniel's shoulders relax, and I force mine to do the same.

"What the hell was that?" I ask as we climb into the car.

"He's a fucking asshole is what that was." Daniel sighs. "We've had disagreements in the past. Nothing that would make him overstep and come after me. Let's go to the club, shall we?"

That thought is nearly enough to drive Christopher from my mind, though I can't help wondering what it was that Katya wanted. The malice I felt from her at the last scene returns to my mind and washes down my spine, hot and sharp. She knows I don't like her. Maybe she knows what I suspected back there. And whether I'm right or wrong, that puts me in a bad position.

I'm about to ask whether she said anything about my absence here last night when Daniel speaks. "What's their next move, Aviva?"

"Sorry?" I think for a moment that he's talking about Katya and Christopher, but realize that's wrong. "You mean the rogues?"

"Precisely. They're mean, but that's no surprise. They're getting what they want by torturing and killing, but there's more. They've gone from quiet killings and leaving the evidence for us to find to going after kids whose parents will not take no for an answer when they report this to the police. Our connections will mean nothing at that point. Not now that the parents can take this to the media. Or social media." He grimaces. We might not use it ourselves, but we're aware how quickly humans can spread ideas, unfiltered and unchecked news, and dangerous truths.I've heard that we have vampires working to counter reports about the supernatural, but we can't control what the living post in a case like this.

I have no idea what's next based on what I've seen of the rogues at the scenes. As far as I can tell they're just enjoying the moment. They won't kill in public. They're too careful about evidence for me to think that any of them will risk being caught in the act. On the other hand, leaving bodies out for all to see doesn't seem outside the realm of possibility.

But why?

Daniel has started the car, but he hasn't backed out of the driveway yet. He's staring into the yard, thinking. "It's like they want us to get found out," he says. "They're testing us, undermining Miranda, showing us our weaknesses."

So what comes next? It seems like we can cover almost anything up, though more bodies will make that hard, and I have no doubt these rogues are laughing at whoever has to deal with this shit. But as long as people have their stories, their mental images of vampires as fictional, they won't believe—

I sit up straight and grab Daniel's arm. "The stock. The next logical step is to go after them."

His muscles tense under my grip, but he waits for me to go on.

My thoughts are murky, but this is obvious. "The

rogues don't need to do this, they *want* to. Which means they see something wrong with the way we do things. They either don't like the current clan system, or they want to..." Shit. I can't think clearly. "I need to feed. But it makes sense, right? If they want panic, if they want to undermine what the elders have built, what better way than to threaten the only living humans who know what we really are?"

Daniel puts the car in reverse, and we're on our way.

Our stock might not consciously think about us between visits. I'm told they tend not to, until the craving gets bad. Even without their memories cleared, things can be hard for them to remember until they've come to us several times. But they know. They expect us to protect them. If we can't, it all goes to hell.

And I think that's exactly where these rogues want us.

We pass a police car on its way into the neighbourhood as we're leaving. No lights, no sirens, but maybe someone checking up on a kid who hasn't been answering messages from absent parents. Probably thinking she's wasting her time, but glad she doesn't have anything more pressing to attend to.

I wonder whether she'll go into the house, find something we missed that tips her off. Even if she doesn't, her life is about to become very complicated.

I know the feeling.

CHAPTER FIFTEEN

T he Inferno is busy tonight, and the stock seem nervous. It's not anything overt, but thin tension runs through the crowd, and they're all seeking company that will relax them when they get the poison they so desperately want. I suspect it's not that they've somehow become aware of the killings, but that they're picking up on the tight expressions and distracted glances of the vampires. There are a lot of us here. Everyone is working hard, and we all need to feed when we can.

Daniel speaks to the bartender, a pretty vampire with red-gold hair, then returns to me. "I'm going to talk to Miranda, let her know what you thought about the stock. I don't know whether the rogues will be that bold, but we'll ensure that everyone is taken care of. The bar is wide open for anyone working on the case. Go feed. You look like shit."

He winks at me and takes off. He's not looking much better than I am, though he still appears stronger, more powerful, and way more beautiful than any of the living humans here tonight. I watch him disappear through the doorway that leads to the back rooms, then turn my attention to the selection of vials behind the bar.

He'll handle this. Miranda will listen to him more than she would to me, and I'm grateful for a few extra minutes to feed.

I choose a vial of light violet liquid that feels promising and search the crowd for someone willing and interested. I don't have to look for long. A young woman with thick black hair raises her eyebrows at me, questioning. I hold my vial up, and she approaches without hesitation.

"Hey!"

A familiar grip takes hold of my shoulder and spins me around. Trixie pulls me into an enthusiastic embrace that leaves me staggering when she lets go. Between my hunger, the lights in here, and Trixie's affectionate attack, I'm getting dizzy. I hold up a finger to my chosen stock to tell her to wait, and she halts in the middle of the floor.

"I miss you so much already," Trixie says, pouting and twirling her pink hair around a finger. "You should come join us. I'm learning so much from Katya." She looks back over her shoulder and scans the crowd. "Not that there's anything wrong with Daniel, but you're as ready for a new teacher as I am, you know?" She's speaking quickly, full of energy I wish I had. She tilts her head. "He's not being too hard on you now that you're his sole target, is he?"

My disorganized mind shifts back to the other day, remembering exactly how hard he was on me, and in spite of my exhaustion warm energy stirs low in my belly. "He's been fine. We're still making progress on my issues."

I'm so hungry I can hardly string a sentence together. My perceptions at that house really drained me. I just want to go. My victim, who's growing more desirable by the second, tilts her head to one side, exposing her throat to me. Flirting.

"Have you eaten?" I ask Trixie.

"I'm good," she says, grinning.

Obviously. I don't know who she fed from, but she looks incredible. Strong, happy, and healthier than I've seen her in a long time. Maybe ever. She looks like I felt the other day with Daniel. "Your new position seems to be agreeing with you."

"So much. Katya's tough, but like I said, so great. I think she'd like to have you with us."

"Really?" That seems so wrong, given what I know about her.

My prey trails long, red nails over her throat and shoots a longing look at another vampire. I clench my teeth. It's all I can do not to abandon Trixie and tackle my victim right here on the dance floor.

"Really. She said you seemed to be picking things up at

the scene the other day. Seemed disappointed that you weren't there last night. But..." She frowns and pouts at the same time, an exaggerated expression that's not out of place on her pretty face. "Are you over what you were thinking before, about her being involved in this?"

"Yeah, yeah." I'm barely listening to Trixie now. Nothing she's saying matters. "We're good."

"Oh, awesome. Anyway, Katya said they found some evidence back at the scene tonight, so maybe we'll be hunting soon. Do think about coming with us, okay? We'd make a great team."

"Sure. I gotta go."

Trixie glances at the woman I can't take my eyes off of and laughs. "Have fun. We'll talk later."

As soon as I'm free, my prey sashays toward me, hips swaying. She's wearing a tight skirt and a sweater that shows off her stomach. She holds up a glass of white wine, and I pour my vial into it.

"Never tried this one," she says, and sips. She giggles. "Oh, wow. That's strong." Her eyes widen, and she glances over her shoulder. "I feel like a butterfly. Am I?"

"If you want to be."

I lead her toward one of the curtained alcoves at the back of the room. A flash of silver-white hair catches my eye, and I slow.

Kayta smiles at me and raises a glass of whatever she's drinking. I nod and try to open myself, but I don't have much energy left to feel her. She looks happy enough. Smug, maybe. Must have had a good meal.

My companion steps up close beside me and strokes her hand down my arm, making circles on the soft fabric of my sweater. "This is nice. Are we goin'?"

We are. She seats herself on a velvet bench. She's not new at this like the young man I had Easter Sunday, but that's fine. The experienced ones can be just as good if they've had time to recharge. Not as bright and full of life, but they know what to expect. Which is perfect, since I'm in no mood to tease her or myself tonight.

She giggles and sips her drink again as I pull the curtains closed. "I never did this with a girl one of you before," she says, rolling her head back to lean against the wall. "Think I'll like it?"

"Only one way to find out." I run my fingers through her dark tresses. She tenses, but only for a moment. Then she sighs and leans into my touch, uncrossing her legs and setting her drink aside. Her scent fills the air. She knows what to expect, anticipates the unique pleasure I can bring her.

I trail a fingernail over her throat as I sit next to her, following the path she showed me out on the floor. She shifts closer to me on the bench, leaning her shoulders in, pulling the neckline of her sweater further down. Her shiver is pure delight as I lean in and wrap an arm around her sturdy waist. When I trace my tongue across the throbbing vein at her throat, she reaches up to tangle her fingers in my hair, trying to pull me closer.

She's overstepping, as they tend to do when the craving is bad.

Her skin is delicate, and offers hardly any resistance to my fangs. She moans softly. "There it is," she sighs.

There it is, I silently agree as her hot blood pulses into my mouth. I wrap one hand around her throat and squeeze, and she gasps as she lets go of my hair. I let my hand drop, trailing over the curves that fill her sweater. She's feeling good. Euphoric from what I put in her drink, excited about this feeding and my touch. I don't need any special gift to feel it. It's all coming to me in her blood. She leans harder against me, shifting as far as she can with my mouth clamped to her neck, and a violent shudder passes through her.

The euphoria is amusing me, but it's not what I came for. The strength is what I want, and it infuses every part of my mind and body as I take her life into myself, bringing clarity and focus where it was missing before. My thoughts are scattered puzzle pieces snapping into their proper places, but all I can think about is her.

It's hard to stop, just as it was with my young man, just as it always is to some degree. Her breathing grows shallow and I draw back, licking away what flows from her wounds. A moment of irrational rage passes through me, disappearing as quickly as it comes. I get this feeling sometimes at the end of a good feeding, like there's something more just around the corner that I'm stopping short of. This is good. Amazing. But the dark void within me screams for whatever peak of existence lies beyond stopping.

I pull away. The feeling will fade. It always does.

She claps a handkerchief to her neck. It won't take long for the bleeding to stop. She shivers again and smiles. Her eyes are unfocused and full of wonder. "Thank you," she whispers. "I think I'm just gonna stay here for a bit."

Daniel is nowhere to be found when I emerge. I ask the bartender whether she's seen him.

She nods toward an alcove not far from mine. "He seemed famished. I don't say he'll be long, now."

She's right. He emerges a minute later and immediately fixes his eyes on me. He heads for a dark corner, and I follow. As soon as we're out of direct view of the rest of the club, he steps up behind me, letting me feel exactly how good his feeding was.

"Nice of you to save that for me," I murmur over my shoulder, and he chuckles against my ear.

"Shall we get out of here?" He trails a hand over the front of my sweater.

"Stock are safe?"

"Miranda has it under control. We're off duty for now. Let's go home."

I doubt we'll make it that far. I feel blood-drunk, coursing with strength and life and the euphoric bliss I induced in my prey even before I gave her what she really wanted. My body is as alive as it can feel from a feeding, and I'm desperate for more. I want Daniel, here, now, filling me and pushing me closer to that unimaginable height that seemed so close just a few minutes ago. The deep throbbing between my legs isn't going to let me ignore it until I'm satisfied.

The stock are fine. Trixie is safe and happy. The world can go on without us for a while.

We hurry up the stairs and out the door, into the shadows of the alley. Daniel pushes me into a dark corner and against the wall, and the world becomes a blur of frenzied kisses and nips, his hands sliding up under my sweater, mine fumbling at his belt. We're definitely not going to make it home. This is stupid, reckless. I know that we should stop, that he should know better and so should I, but I don't care.

He freezes, snarls in my ear, and steps back, straightening his clothes. I do the same, unsure what's happening until I regain my composure and sense the power that has exited the club and is approaching us. Two pairs of footsteps. No attempt to hide. I guess I should be glad of that.

"Good evening, Katya," Daniel says, voice husky, sounding maybe half as irritated as I suspect he actually is. "Christopher."

Katya gives us a slow grin and comes to a stop just out of arm's reach. Her friend leaves us less space. Daniel takes a half step forward, halting Christopher's approach. "What can we do for you?"

Katya fixes her eyes on me. That air of satisfaction hasn't left her, but it feels far less benign now that I realize it has something to do with me. The malice I felt from her before swirls through her power now, bright and predatory. She's a cat toying with her prey, and I have no idea what I've done.

My conversation with Trixie comes back to me. *Are you over what you were thinking before, about her being involved in this?*

My blood chills. I never told Trixie what I thought about that. Katya must have. She knows.

Shit.

"Stand aside, Daniel," Katya says, practically purring. "Aviva is wanted for questioning in the matter of the rogue killings."

"That's absurd. She was nowhere near the crime scenes when the murders happened."

Katya raises an eyebrow. "I'm sure you'll be able to go into great detail about where she was on those occasions, won't you? Don't make this difficult for yourself, Daniel. If she's innocent, I'm sure we'll figure that out soon enough, without your help." She raises an eyebrow at him. "You have enough black marks on your record already. Don't make it worse."

So calm. So reasonable. And I don't believe a word of

it. She'll have me locked up before I can blink, and we don't have anything like a right to a lawyer in our world. She won't hesitate to drag Daniel's reputation through the mud if he stands in her way. If he thought he had it bad when he got demoted to training the likes of me and Trixie, I can't imagine what another misstep will do to him.

"I want you to go with them, Aviva," he says.

My chest hitches. I can't even answer.

"Trust your elders," he adds. "Katya will take care of you."

Something presses into my hand, the one that's hidden behind his back. His wallet. I slip it into my pocket, and he pushes against my hip.

I don't need another hint. I turn and run.

"Aviva, wait!" Daniel hollers. There's a crashing noise behind me, Christopher's low voice swearing, and the sound of footsteps. Three sets.

"There's nowhere you can hide!" Katya calls.

I don't look back. There's a dark night and a big city out there waiting to shelter me. I'm willing to take my chances.

CHAPTER SIXTEEN

God, I'm hungry.

It's been six days. There was enough cash in Daniel's wallet for me to get a room in a cheap motel in Paradise that's so quiet and dismal I suspect it's a front for something else. There's no way this place does enough actual business to stay open.

I've had a lot of time this week to consider that idea. It's not like I can go anywhere I might be seen. I can't go home. Haven't tried to contact Daniel. Yes, he gave me his wallet, he pushed me to go. But he obviously wants them to think he's on their side, and I don't know how far that goes. I don't even know whether he's under suspicion. Katya's not stupid. If she thinks he knows where I am or that he's trying to help me, he might be in shit as deep as I am right now.

I don't want that. Maybe he's talked her down. Convinced her I don't think she did it.

Not that I'm convinced anymore that she *is* innocent. Why would she turn on me if she wasn't guilty? Surely it's not because she feels threatened by me as some kind of future rival. I've tried to give that angle a shot. Considered that maybe she picked up on what I was doing at that murder scene when I first suspected her and feels threatened by the potential of my gift. Or maybe threatened by my relationship with Daniel. But that's ridiculous.

There's no scenario where her coming after me when she's not guilty makes sense. I just wish I thought anyone else would see it that way.

If, as Trixie said, Katya did notice me picking something up, she'll probably frame it as me being a danger to everyone. Somehow. Especially now that I'm on the loose and hungry. She's got to be painting me as untrustworthy by now, which will only make it less likely that anyone will believe me without hard evidence against her. Even if I tell what I know, if I reveal how I know it, it's not going to help my case.

The upshot of it all is that I'm no longer doubting what I saw that day. Her shadow prowling around as that woman begged for her life, as her husband tried to fight. Her loving gaze cast over her fine meal. Those weren't rookie mistakes caused by my dislike of Katya. I understand now that it was truth that came from my gift—a truth

I dismissed. I'm not going to make that mistake again, even if no one else ever believes me.

She came after me hard and fast because she knew no one would question her judgement. She's not interested in bringing me down a peg or two. She wants me finished, pinned as a rogue, executed.

She's guilty, and she's afraid of what I saw.

I can't leave town. Not when Trixie could be facing a danger she's completely blind to. Not when there's still a chance I can help, if only I can figure out how.

And definitely not when I'm out of cash. Between this shitty, water-stained room and the coffees I keep running out to get in the early evening when my hunters are less likely to be around, I'm just about broke.

It's night now, but the hunger is bad, and I need another hit of caffeine to keep me going if I can't get anything stronger. I saw a diner down by the industrial area up the street that might be open late. It's off the main road. Maybe if I keep my wits about me I can keep from getting caught.

It's raining when I step out of my ground floor room, a light drizzle that leaves the stars invisible. I take a deep breath, letting the night air fill and cleanse me. I haven't been physically active, save for the little walking I've done and the training exercises I've been able to keep up with in my room. It's not physical exhaustion that's got me longing for blood now, but time and stress. Sleepless days. An unending merry-go-round of discarded ideas about what the hell I'm going to do now.

Maybe I'll have to go back and throw myself on Miranda's mercy. Daniel will speak for me. I think. I hope. Even if he doesn't, maybe they'll give me a last meal before they finish me for good. Pretty soon I'll be so hungry that the threat of eternal oblivion will seem a small price to pay for warm blood flooding my mouth.

I'm drooling. Fuck.

I turn my collar up against the drizzle and make my way down the street, ducking through back streets as soon as I can to stay out of sight of street traffic.

The empty diner is open and lit up inside, though the sign outside is only halfway there, boasting "DI R" with the occasional flicker of a ghostly E. A small dark shape sits hunched outside the door. As I approach, the shorthaired cat with a torn ear lifts its head and shoots me a disdainful glare from golden eyes set into a face covered in black and white inky blotches. The cat stretches as I reach for the door and darts ahead of me as a cheerful bell announces our presence.

The pretty brunette girl behind the counter, maybe eighteen years old and dressed in a turquoise uniform straight out of a 50's diner, straightens from her position hunched over a textbook. "Rory, you can't be in here," she tells the cat.

It ignores her, leaping up onto the counter and lying down, blinking at me.

"I won't tell anyone if you won't," I say. My voice is rough. I haven't used it much this week.

The girl, whose nametag reads *Imogen*, offers me a tense little smile. I must look like shit, and she probably doesn't get the highest-class clientele in here. I won't stay and make her nervous. "Coffee to go, please," I say, setting my last fiver on the counter. "Black."

"You got it." She closes the book—advanced chemistry —and grabs a large paper cup that she fills to the top from the pot on the counter behind her. It smells like heaven and probably tastes like shit, but it will do its job.

The door jingles again, and a draft of cold air cuts through the warmth of the diner. The waitress looks over, and her expression tightens. A man reaches for one of the plastic menus displayed on the eat-in counter, dripping rainwater from his sleeve everywhere. He's looking at us, not at the prices, watery blue eyes darting between the girl's hemline and my face.

"Working alone tonight, sweetie?" he asks the girl.

"No. Brock's in the kitchen until close."

"Huh. Bad night to be out for a walk," he says, nodding at my wet jacket. Apparently he's given her up as a target. That's something, at least.

I accept my coffee and a few bucks change from the waitress, but I don't move toward the door. She might not have been too sure about me, but I've got to be better than being alone with this guy. I sip my coffee. It's better than I expected, full and rich and hot. I'm tired enough that it tastes like pure, restorative magic.

He orders what I have and leans on the counter, eyes raking over me, making my skin crawl. "I've got an umbrella in my car if you want it," he says.

"No, thanks. I'm fine."

He shoots me a grin that's probably supposed to be charming but comes off as a grimace. "Not made of sugar, are you?"

"Sorry?"

"Not going to melt in the rain. Sure are sweet, though."

I roll my eyes and look away. The waitress catches my eye and smiles in sympathy. I turn my back to the man and look over a bulletin board covered in outdated flyers, hoping he'll take the hint. After a long minute, the bell jingles. In my peripheral vision I catch Imogen shooting what I can only assume is a high school attempt at the evil eye after him, muttering something foul under her breath.

I kind of like her.

The cat lets out a low rumble as the guy passes by the big plate glass window and disappears into the night.

"Me too, buddy," I say quietly, and Imogen smiles.

"You need anything else?" she asks. "Pie? On the house."

"No, thanks. I should be going. Take care."

I don't try to pet the cat on my way out. He looks like a scrapper.

Three blocks later I'm deep in a warren of streets lined with warehouses, enjoying the night. I know I should go back. I'm too exposed out here, and I'd be a fool if I thought the hunters weren't still looking for me. They know I'm broke and can't go far, even if Daniel tells them I stole his wallet. But it's good to be out. I belong to the night, and I can't enjoy it if I'm cooped up.

I don't pray anymore. I can no longer bask in the warmth I used to feel from it. But the night fills me and renews me in a different way, and if I want to survive, I need this. The night sky is my cathedral ceiling now.

A long, high-pitched whistle sounds behind me. I don't stop or turn back, even at the sound of multiple sets of footsteps splashing over the asphalt.

Humans. Bring it on, guys.

They slow slightly, probably confused by my non-reaction. I was supposed to look back at them, maybe run.

They're obviously not afraid, though. Stupid creatures.

"Hey, sugar," calls a familiar voice. "Bad night. Bad neighbourhood to be alone in. Need company?"

"Fuck off."

Another voice laughs, and they keep coming. I turn down an alley, and they follow. Dead end.

"You fellas looking for a party or something? I'm not in the mood." I turn to face them. They're standing three abreast, tallest one in the middle. The skinny fellow from the diner stands to his left, and a squat guy with a face like a rotten jack-o'-lantern is on his right. All wear warm coats, the tallest in plaid, the others black. They look every bit as scrappy as that cat did earlier, but I won't be leaving these guys in peace. I might be starving, but I'm still a vampire, and I haven't had a chance to stretch my legs properly in almost a week.

These guys have no idea what they've walked into.

The one from the diner steps forward and produces a knife from his pocket. "Stay quiet, and we won't hurt you."

I laugh. "Bullshit."

"Empty your pockets, miss. Hand over your wallet."

I reach for my pocket and trace the worn leather weight that's rested there since I ran from Daniel. "I would, but it's not mine. So very sorry."

Jack-o'-Lantern scrunches his face tighter. "What?"

"The answer is no." I stand with my arms at my sides, relaxed. All three take hesitant steps forward, but seem at a loss. "So what's it going to be? I don't want trouble." That's a lie, but I should give them a chance to go. I'm on edge, pissed off, and I can't guarantee I'll remember how fragile they are if it comes to a fight. I'm not used to sparring with the living. I don't want to kill them.

Diner Guy shifts his weight onto one leg and then the other, shuffling forward, knife gripped confidently. "We're not bluffing."

"Neither am I."

The second he's in range, Diner Guy finds himself face-down in a puddle with his arm twisted behind him and one of my knees pressed into the small of his back.

He screams, and I ease the pressure on his arm so I don't rip it out of the socket. The thick, sickly scent of fear fills the alley. That, and piss. I twist his wrist and catch the knife in my other hand, then use it to motion for the others to come closer so I don't have to speak too loudly.

"You boys are making really poor life choices, you know that?"

The two look at each other. Tall Man nods, and they both run forward, hollering.

I stand and deliver a sharp kick to Diner Guy's side to keep him down, then hit Tall Man with an uppercut that sends him flying into the side of a dumpster. His buddy Jack-o-Lantern pulls a switchblade and launches himself at me, and I spin out of the way. He stumbles and hits the pavement hard. I kick him in the shin while he's down, and he screams. I could easily take them all out with the knife in my hand, but I'm not ready for that.

Diner Guy gets up and rushes at me, yelling something unintelligible.

"Shut up!" I yell. I grab him by the lapels of his filthy coat and catch his cheek with the edge of his knife as I spin him away.

One of the others groans.

"I said shut up." My head is swimming. I'm not weak. Not yet. But having my perceptions and movements in high gear is taking it out of me. "*Stay quiet* was your rule, not mine. At least abide by it."

Diner Guy is bleeding from the deep cut on his cheek, and the thick scent of blood fills the alley. "You bitch," he mutters.

God, that smell. I can't even think anymore. I lunge at him and pin him against the concrete wall opposite the dumpster.

He struggles, but can't move with his arms trapped behind him. I lean in closer, drawn by the blood that promises strength and clarity. There's no thought. No decision. I'm all instinct now, and as far as I've ever been from the humanity I cling to. I grab his hair with my free hand and force his face hard against the wall. My tongue travels up his cheek, over the flap of skin that lies loose.

Tremors of pleasure shoot through me, and my power roars to life. I taste his fear, his helplessness. It escalates as I release a predator's snarl. His fear fills me, urging me on, pulling me closer to that height of experience I've denied myself so many times. I trail my nails over his throat.

My mouth waters, but my venom doesn't seem to be doing anything to soothe him. He's beyond any place where he could potentially enjoy this.

Good.

It would be so easy, so fulfilling, to sink my fangs into

him. I need his blood, and the world would be better off without this piece of shit wandering its streets.

Movement catches my eye. Tall Man is up on his feet, staring at me.

"What... what the hell are you doing?" He sounds horrified, like he's just seen a real monster for the first time, and it's far worse than what he imagined under his bed when he was a kid.

He backs away, joined by Jack-o-Lantern, who's crawling. I think I broke his leg.

Diner Guy starts to cry. "P-please," he stutters.

I drag my tongue across the cut again and tighten my fingers around his throat. As his fear for his life spikes, his taste changes. This is what I've craved without knowing it since I died, what safe and pleasant feedings have only mostly satisfied. Trixie had the right idea, after all. Fear and pain are incredible. Exotic. *Right*.

Trixie. Katya.

No.

I step back, releasing him. He doesn't need encouragement to run. They're all gone a few seconds later, Jack-o-Lantern helped along by his buddies.

I stand in the dark alley, trembling. It wasn't a proper feeding, and this strength won't last long. But God, I feel incredible. Not warm or pleasant, but *here*. One with the night, with my power, like I've never been before. I want to howl, to run, to fight, to claim the city for myself.

I give my head a hard shake. I have to go. If those guys breathe a word of this, my enemies will hear about it. They'll know where to find me. Maybe they already do, if that fight was as loud as I think it was.

I need to go.

My thoughts race faster than my legs as they push me over dark streets. What did I just do?

What would I have done if I'd been alone with him, if we hadn't been interrupted?

I can't get that hungry again. That monstrous thing within me won't rest until I feed, and I won't let it happen out here on the streets again. One way or another, this has to end.

Daniel said no one would ever believe me without hard evidence. Fine.

I turn and head east, back toward the place where this all began.

CHAPTER SEVENTEEN

The Kilbride house is quiet. No sign of human interference, no police tape. Either these people didn't have the type of friends that would notice them going missing, or Maelstrom is even better at cover-ups than I ever realized.

The back door is locked now, but subtlety's not my aim tonight. I break the lock and close the door behind me. It doesn't quite catch, but from outside the place should look quiet. That's all I need. I'm not staying long.

The kitchen is clean. It's a relief and a disappointment all at once. I still smell a hint of stale blood, but no human who came in here would know that anything happened. The table is gone, as is the laundry basket from the stairs.

I breathe in the bleach-tainted air. There's nothing here for me, as far as I can tell. With the bodies and blood gone, it's deader than the last place. My heart feels like it's deflating, but I can't give up now. I'm here. I have nothing but this house and the power that's still stirring within me. They'll have to be enough if I want to see another sunset.

I wonder what will happen to me if I'm caught. Every night that's passed without me turning myself in has probably sealed my fate more firmly. I'm not trustworthy. What happened in that alley tonight will count as endangering our secrets.

I hope it's quick. I've heard rogues get a needle. Something that takes them out instantly, though that's not to say they might not be tortured first.

And that's it for us. No white light. No peaceful rest. I don't have a soul that will live on anymore, for better or worse. This is it. It took me a long time to believe that, but I do now, just as firmly as I once believed in heaven.

I tighten my fists until my nails dig into the palms of my hands and the pain brings me back to the present.

This *is* it. This moment is all I have. My life is over. My future is in question. If I'm going to learn anything that will bring the rogues and Katya to justice, it happens now.

The tastes of blood and fear linger on my tongue, exciting my power. At least that's something. I just need to find a way to connect with these people again.

I ignored the shadows when I was here before. I'm ready to listen now, if it's not too late.

I rifle through the open mail on the desk in the living room. Bills, some of them second notices. But she just had the windows done. Either things aren't as bad as they look, or she was getting the place ready to sell. I want it to be the former. Maybe she was just careless.

The desk drawers don't offer much else, and I turn my attention to the shelves by the TV. Three baby books, one pink, one blue, one yellow. The pink one is pretty full at the beginning, sparse after a few years. The next one shows good effort, too. The third one has barely been touched. Cute babies, I guess. I was never great with little kids. I don't dislike them, though, and the thought of these bright little beings facing what they did claws at my heart.

I wonder whether this mother would have made different choices if she'd known how things would end, or whether their short lives were better than nothing. I want to obey my old orders and turn my thoughts away from that, look at things objectively, but I don't. This is okay. This is how I'll learn more.

Or not. There's not even a hint of a shadow here, no matter how hard I think about these kids or their mom. Not even as I walk back through the kitchen. Everything is cleaned up. They're gone.

I wander up the dark staircase, passing a gallery of framed pictures. The girl grins in school photos for kindergarten to grade three. The boy wore glasses. He didn't have those on when he died.

The atmosphere upstairs weighs heavier on me, and my steps slow. It's faint, but there's something. No one has cleaned up here. The space is still tainted, by fear if not by blood.

Did I say I don't pray anymore? I can't help it now. I don't address it, but a silent plea goes out to whoever might be listening.

If not for me, for them. Please.

The bedroom at the top of the stairs is small, just big enough for a double bed that hardly leaves enough room for closet doors and dresser drawers to open. I sit on the edge of the unmade bed and think about the mother. The faint scent of her clings to the sheets. I lie down and rest my head on the pillow.

The flood of emotion comes fast and hard. Confusion, terror... not for herself alone, but for her children. If I thought my heart was being clawed at before, this is ripping it in two.

The connection is exhausting, but it's coming.

Laughter. The rogues do enjoy their work.

Shadows.

The door bursts open, flooding the room with blinding light. Impossibly strong hands haul her out of bed. She tries to fight them off, scratching and kicking, and they laugh again. She begs them to leave the children alone, she'll do whatever they want. A cold hand clamps over her mouth.

I sit up. I can't see anything helpful, and if I linger in her mind I'll go insane.

But I can't shake her.

I stagger out into the hallway, and the shadows follow. Black and white images, faded like old photos.

Chills pass over my skin as I catch sight of an after-image about to fade. A slim form walking ahead, white hair swaying as she moves.

They're gone, and I can't call them back, even when I force myself to return to the bed and lie down. The mother's shadows are gone, but I got what I needed for myself.

My gift never lied to me. Katya wasn't in London when these crimes happened. She was right here.

Bile rises in my throat, and I lean forward on the bed to rest my head between my knees as white spots pass from my vision. The hell of this now is that I'm no closer to proving a damned thing than I was before. Daniel might believe me. Maybe. But even if he does, it won't help. This is no romance that will lead to him throwing himself on enemy swords to save me. He's walking a tightrope right now, and anyway, I'm not such a terrible loss. Even if he misses me for a while, that's nothing to a creature who will live centuries. I'm a blip in his experience.

I don't want to die again. I don't want this to be all there is for me.

I force myself to my feet. No one's coming to save me. This is all on me now, and sitting here on my ass isn't going to help.

I'm still staggering, even without emotion crowding my mind. I'm going to have to be careful. The other crime scenes didn't drain me like this. But then, I wasn't this weak going into them, and I wasn't working this hard.

The scrap of me that still feels connected to life and light feels strong. Awake. I cling to that as I move down the hall and enter a larger bedroom. This difference, this mistake in my makeup, is just about all I have left.

Bunk beds in here, with a pink comforter on the bottom bunk and blue on the top. Two dressers, one desk, and a door to the ensuite bathroom. Mom gave the older kids the master bedroom.

A yellow binder on the desk tells me as much about the girl as a diary would. The margins of the notes are filled with the initials "KB+JS" in hearts, and her name in various forms. Kari Black. Kari Smith. Kari Black-Smith. There's a giant question mark and exclamation point on both sides of that last one.

Third grade and the kid already had a sense of humour I appreciate.

I close the notes and lie on the bottom bunk. My little friend Kari was already awake when they came in. Tears stream down my face, and I can't help the sob that escapes as I close my eyes and the shadows crowd in. Her thoughts ring as clear as her emotions, if more fractured and faint.

Big men and two ladies. So scary. They hurt her when they pull her out of bed, like that time Mark Peters gave her what he called an Indian burn but she knows you're not supposed to call it that. She cries. Fear spikes. She screams at them to leave her brother alone. Big gorilla arms scoop her out of bed and haul her out of the room.

Christopher. It has to be.

I pull her pillow to my chest and hold it tight as the shadows fade, just as the mother's did. I can see what happened in a jumble of mixed perceptions, but no matter how real I make it, I can't change anything.

I'm so sorry, Kari.

The upper bunk is just as painful, and no more helpful. I get a vague sense of faces in deep shadow, all of them terribly blurry. They dropped this kid on the floor, broke his arm. I wonder whether our forensics crew gave a damn about that.

I'm trembling all over as I head to the last bedroom, which is painted blue with stick-on truck images on the walls and an economy-size box of size five diapers in the corner. It smells like baby powder on the surface, undercut with the hint of diaper stink that hovers in every nursery no matter how clean it is. I open the big window wide to let some night air in.

I hesitate as I reach out to touch the side bar of the wooden crib. I can already taste the fear at the back of my throat.

I think of this family, the couple in their bedroom, the teenagers in Mount Pearl. If I don't finish this, the rogues will likely be allowed to go back into hiding, only to kill again when they choose to emerge again somewhere else.

One more time, and then I'm done. My fingers grip the rail tight, and I dig deep into both parts of myself—my humanity and my raw, dark power.

The emotions are strong, but confusing. Primitive. The faces that enter the room are blurred, and I can't understand the words I hear. The screams from downstairs are clearer.

The baby started to cry then.

He knows his mama's voice, but it sounds bad. He wants her, screams for her, and she doesn't come. These people smell and feel wrong. Cold. They're not family, and he screams louder. The people laugh, but it's not happy like when mama plays with him. A mass of white hair swirls around him as someone reaches down to pick him up. He tries to brush the hair away, but it gets tangled in his fingers where they're sticky from him sucking on them as he fell asleep. He pulls his hand back, and she flinches. She pinches him hard under his arm, and the pain is a shock shooting through his body. He reaches for his teddy bear and catches it by the arm, but it's jostled out of his hand as they haul him away from his bed, and he cries harder.

I look around for the teddy bear. There's a little blue one propped on the dresser, but it's not the same. The one I saw was larger, brown, with curly fur. I want it. If that was his favourite toy, it might tell me more. Maybe. I don't even know. My thoughts are muddling again.

I just need that fucking bear. The thought is as instinctive as my desire to feed earlier.

I push myself away from the crib, search the dresser drawers and the closet, but it's gone. They must have taken it when they cleaned up after themselves.

That's it. I'm fucked.

I sink to the floor, used up and worn out. I can't do any more here. Katya has been committing the perfect crimes, and she won't get caught until she wants to.

Maybe I can still leave town and regroup. Get Trixie and Daniel to come with me, if I can convince them of what I saw. It's nowhere near proof, but—

He pulled her hair. Hard. That's why she pinched him.

I press my face to the side of the crib mattress. I just need a little more.

Teddy fell behind, and he's gone. Mama gets mad when Teddy falls back there, because it's hard to reach him out. It was a fun game until the time Mama took Teddy away because—

That's all. It's gone.

It's enough.

I'm on my stomach, lifting the ruffled skirt and squirming under the crib. The shadows are almost black under here. There's nothing on the floor, but something is hanging down, trapped between the mattress and the slats on the far side. I tug gently, and a little bear falls into my hand.

Of course it's small. It looked big in his mind because *he* was small.

I choke back a sob of mixed grief and anger.

Tangled around Teddy's furry arm is a single long, white hair.

I laugh through my tears. I can't help it.

I stand on shaky legs and clutch the bear tight, careful to keep the hair intact and attached. This proves that Katya was here, and she can't claim she lost the hair during the investigation.

She was in London for this one, or so she says.

I turn to find a phone to call Daniel, and pause. The world outside these rooms disappeared while I was lost in the shadows, but it's coming back to me. Nothing is clear. I'm almost powerless now.

But nothing can mask the sharp, red anger that's approaching.

Katya appears in the doorway, smiling. She's still feeling smug and satisfied, like she was back at the club, but there's a wild fury in it now. She prowls in, a cat on the hunt, graceful and filled with a power that radiates from her. She's been inducing fear, killing. I've only had a taste of that, but based on what I felt in that alley, I imagine she's far stronger now than she's ever let anyone but the other rogues see.

I have no chance against her.

"I knew you'd come back," she says. "You're smart. Talented. I'm sorry we didn't meet sooner, when I might have helped you."

She sounds like she means it, but she still hates me. I can feel that. She wants to hurt me, and I don't think that means turning me in. Not when I've seen what I have here tonight.

I turn, intending to throw myself out the window, but she's on me before I can take a step. I expect to feel pain.

Instead, a needle pierces my arm, and everything disappears into darkness.

CHAPTER EIGHTEEN

Dark.

So cold.

I twist my prone body as I struggle to remember what's happened, but I can't get up. My arms are tied behind me. No, cuffed. The frigid metal digs into my wrists when I try to pull free. I can't see anything through the tight band of cloth covering my eyes.

Every movement feels heavy and slow. I haven't felt this sluggish since before I died, like I haven't slept in days.

I suspect, though, that it's the opposite, and I've slept too much. I don't know how long I've been out. It's harder to judge when you don't dream. Sleep is just a blank, black hole in the day. But all of the strength I gained from my taste of blood in that filthy alley is gone.

I scrape the side of my face against the rough floor I'm lying on and work the blindfold down. No one has gagged me, but I'm not about to speak. Not until I figure out where I am.

Where Katya brought me. My head is muzzy and my thoughts seem to have congealed into a semisolid lump, but I remember that. Her bright eyes, her victorious smile. A lunge. A pinprick.

I should probably be glad I woke up at all. She might have access to whatever it is they use to put rogues like her down for good.

It's dark in here. It smells like a garage. I'm surrounded by walls of boxes that form a wide cell around me, so I can't get a sense of how large the space might be. A cluck of my tongue echoes faintly beyond the stacks. Big space. Maybe a warehouse.

The gasoline stink is nauseating, and worse for the hunger that's waking within me like a yawning pit.

I roll my head from side to side, loosening my neck, then open my mouth to stretch my jaw muscles. They're tight and sore on the left. I don't remember the guys in the alley getting any good shots in. Katya must have taken out her frustrations on me after I went down. Or Christopher, if he was helping her.

Fuckers.

Dull pain thuds behind my eyes, and I lie still until it quiets a little.

Shoulders next, as far as I can move. I'm stiff as a true corpse, but I can work that out if I'm careful and quiet.

The cuffs won't let me bring my arms forward, and my feet are tied, but I can at least stretch and flex a little.

Something tugs at the hem of my jeans, and I kick out. It skitters away.

The chill of this place has worked its way into my bones. I want to stretch and pace to rid myself of it, but I doubt I'd have the energy for that even if I could free my hands.

I roll onto my side and use the momentum to shift to a sitting position with my hands behind me, barely keeping myself from toppling over again. The room swirls and tips sideways, and I close my eyes until the dizziness passes. When it does, I look up toward a ceiling lit by faint security lights. I feel like I should be able to see more. My senses are as sapped as my strength, and I'm reduced to nearly human levels of perception.

How did I live like this? I'd almost forgotten how forbidding shadows can be.

Catwalks span the ceiling high above me. They're narrow, with thin handrails along the sides. Chains and ropes hang from the sides in places. It doesn't tell me much about where I am.

I'm as strong as I'm going to get here. Guess it's time to say hello and hope she hasn't left me here to waste away. I think she hasn't. If she wanted to finish me, she'd have done it. We're not through yet, Katya and I.

"Katya!" I shout. My voice cracks.

A door opens and closes somewhere beyond the boxes, and hard-soled boots clop across the floor. She's not moving as lightly as she was when she sneaked up on me, but there's a strength I can only envy in those steps.

She shoves a stack of boxes aside, sending them cascading to the floor with thuds that echo, beating into my head like drums and bringing my headache roaring back. I don't react to the noise, or to the faint sunlight that streams into my space from high, filthy windows that were blocked from view before. Not enough to hurt me if I was at full strength, but right now it's not doing good things for the pain.

On the surface, Katya looks as composed as she ever has. Low-heeled boots, dark jeans that look like they were cut just to fit her, tailored jacket. But the blouse underneath is wrinkled, like she's slept in it, and her hair's tied up in a high ponytail. She sets her hands on her hips and purses her lips as she looks me over.

"You're awake."

I don't know how to answer that, so I stare up at her, waiting.

She chuckles. "How are we feeling today?"

"Like shit." I don't have the strength to lie. I wish I had an ounce of Trixie's attitude to offer her.

"You didn't like my medicine?" She crouches well outside of my reach and rests her elbows on her knees. "That was a little taste of true death. Just a drop, and diluted, but you've been out for three days. Any more and you'd be gone completely, never to return. This is what we do to traitors and criminals."

"Like you?"

She grins, fangs gleaming in the faint light. "Yet here I am, and soon you won't be. So what are we to make of that?"

The room swims again. "You're setting me up?"

She shrugs and stands. "We'll see how well you play the game."

"What?" I can't follow what she's saying. I need a drink. I need blood. I need something. "Why are you doing all of this?"

Her lip lifts in a gorgeous sneer. "You'll understand some day, Aviva, if I let you survive that long. You'll see how boring it all gets after a few centuries. How you work for something great, only to see it fall flat and become a pathetic imitation of what you intended."

"Maelstrom." My mouth feels like it's full of dry cotton, and I can barely get the word out.

She nods and kicks a box aside. "And all of the clans. We worked so hard to create our own world. A place where we could be safe, where we could exist alongside the living without drawing them out to hunt us as we slept unaware and unguarded. Do you know how low our numbers got before Miranda and I began working on this little project? How vulnerable we were in the old days?"

I don't answer. My history lessons are in my head somewhere, but I can't access them. Nothing is connecting.

"Our new world was good at first," she says. "There are so many now who have known nothing else. Who have never killed." She shakes her head. "It works, and we are safe, but the cost is unbearable at times. We're not made to hide. We are hunters, not farmers. Mere survival is not what we were created for. I didn't see that before."

She seems to be talking more to herself than to me.

"Does Miranda agree with you? The other elders?"

She snorts and focuses her attention on me again. "No. And it's certainly not something I'm likely to bring up in a meeting. As far as they know, I'm loyal. And I am their best hunter, aren't I?" She laughs, surprisingly gently. "I have the best of both worlds, and that's what I offer those closest to me. Those I see potential in. Those I trust." She tilts her head, observing me carefully. "Have you tasted fear, Aviva?"

"Yes."

"Death?"

"Never."

She nods slowly. "I suspect that may be part of your problem. I remember when you were made, how angry the elders were. So unsuited. And you didn't prove us wrong, did you? Clinging to life as though you had even a scrap of a soul remaining. Refusing to feed for far too long. Moaning over your loss when you had been given so much." There's something like pity in her eyes. "It's cases like yours where bending the laws about killing would benefit us so much. There was a time when a newly turned vampire would be forced to starve for days, then allowed to hunt. No half measures there. No question of what we were. Just the joy of a starved body being flooded with life, and a clean break. Wouldn't that have been better than your sad little preoccupation with life?"

"No."

She grins. "I thought you'd say that. You really do look like shit, you know. Probably almost as bad as you feel. I can fix that for you. One moment."

She leaves me, and I take the opportunity to regroup. She's not offering up this information because she wants conversation. I just wish she'd tell me what the hell she wants.

Muffled cries ring through the warehouse, and my stomach drops as my mouth begins to water.

No. Please.

Katya drags a healthy-looking young man in jeans and a tank top into my makeshift cell by one arm. He's tied like I am, hands and feet, but he's gagged instead of blind-folded. He stares at me with wide, terrified eyes as Katya dumps him on the floor in front of me. He struggles for a moment, then freezes. His sweat fills the air with the musk of fear, and I'm so hungry I can smell the blood in him even with my dulled senses.

I'm aware of my fangs, my sharp venom, and the little strength that remains in my body. It's an instinctive reaction that goes deeper than what I felt in the alley. Did I think I was hungry then? Was I pleased that I had the willpower to stop myself?

I had no idea what hunger was.

"Go ahead," Katya says, and nudges him with her foot.

I turn my face away. If I start, I won't stop.

She pulls a box cutter from her pocket, clicks it up, and nicks his bicep. I can't help but look. Just a little slice, a narrow line of blood that glistens brighter than it should in this dull light. It fills my senses until there's nothing else.

I don't move. I won't.

"This is what you were made for, Aviva. Not constrained half feedings in clubs that cater to the comfort of your victims." She leans over him and inhales deeply. "I'd take him myself, but I have an offer to make you."

The man whimpers, and Katya rolls her eyes as she swats him on the back of the head. "He dies either way. Don't get any ideas about that. The question is whether you walk out of here."

"Why?" My question is a whisper. It's all I can manage.

"Because Daniel's not wrong about you, even if he's gone about your training completely wrong. Especially lately. You have potential of a depth that troubles me. Your perceptions are strange. I don't like it, not least because you seem determined to spoil my little game with what you've seen. But perhaps if you saw things my way, we might work together. If there's one like you, there could be more, and my team will need someone like you to help us understand them."

"What game?"

She frowns. "The only one there has ever been, the only one that makes things interesting. This is why vampires found guilty of crimes are turned out instead of being imprisoned or finished."

"I don't—"

"The hunt, Aviva. We are hunters. Some of us feel that pull more strongly than others. We're no longer allowed to hunt our prey, but hunting rogues? Absolutely. I suspect it's the only way your dear Daniel has managed to keep his impulses under control for so long. He feels it, you know. The urge to kill. To fight. But he's so devoted to Maelstrom and its laws that he'll never go rogue. Not as long as he gets to hunt his own kind. To him it's a job. To me, it's a game I helped create. Sporting. They do get away sometimes."

My stomach is cramping, my mind reeling from the blood that's so close, so available. I force my mind back to her words.

"If it all works so well for you, why rock the boat?" I ask. "You're baiting your own hunters with these kills. Begging them to hunt you down. Threatening to expose all of us and tear down what you built."

"The game gets dull, Aviva. We were in no danger of getting caught, though you did make me wonder about that. Briefly. It's terribly pleasant when the chaos we belong to throws a new complication out into the world, isn't it?" She's grinning again, almost laughing. "So we tease. We approach the line without crossing. Throw out challenges to the system that protects us, risk our very being. Otherwise, what's the point? We're no better than animals in captivity if we don't respect our true natures."

I don't understand. All I can think about now is this man on the floor, shivering with fright and cold. My own muscles tremble, but it's with anticipation. I can't help it. This isn't like living hunger, which goes away if you ignore it long enough, even as it weakens you. This grows deeper with every passing moment, and just the scent of him calls to my power, fills me with enough energy that I know I could take him.

"Explain what you want," I demand, not taking my eyes off him.

"Feed."

"No."

She leans in close. "You will, one way or another. And either you will see things my way, as I suspect you will, or I'll finish you, and you'll take the blame for this murder. Maybe some of the others. Your alibi is weaker than you realize."

"No."

She snarls and stands again. "Trixie!"

My heart leaps into my throat as another set of footsteps hurries toward us.

"Aviva!" Trixie drops to the floor beside me and gathers me in her arms, holding me tight whether I like it or not.

"Katya's a rogue," I gasp as she squeezes me.

"I know." Trixie strokes my hair, pushing it back from my face. "It's not like you think, though. Please listen to her. I had to beg her to give you this chance. Don't waste it, okay?"

I stare at her, not believing what I'm hearing.

"Katya saw my potential the second we met, and she agrees about yours, but you have to listen. Not everyone gets this opportunity. Daniel won't. He couldn't understand this. But I really think you will, and then we'll work together again. It will be great."

"Daniel," I whisper.

"That's over, obviously," Katya says, motioning for Trixie to stand with her. My friend obeys without question. "He'll be safe enough once you move out and come with us. Getting involved with your trainer was quite tasteless, Aviva. I'll expect better of you. Not to mention it will be easier for you to keep our little secret if you're not fucking him."

Trixie giggles.

She knew about Katya. I don't know for how long, but she knew. My only friend.

Katya slashes at the man's arm again, deeper. The blood flows strong and fast now, spilling onto the floor. Hot rage pushes up in me at the sight of it being wasted. He whimpers. I'm beyond caring.

Katya winds her fingers into the hair at the back of his head and lifts him as though he weighs no more than a doll. He squirms, and she hits him in the side of the head. He collapses, dazed but not quite unconscious, and she makes a tiny slit in his throat with the box cutter. His pulse throbs beneath the cut, pushing bright blood out in a thin stream.

"Eat," she orders. "This is life. Take it."

She drops the cutter and grabs me as she did him, and I'm too weak to fight as she pushes my mouth to his throat. My fangs pierce his skin, biting hard and deep, releasing the flood. He feels it. I know he does, because his terror spikes, filling my mouth with something richer and deeper than blood alone. It pushes all thought from my mind.

A click of a lock behind me, and my hands are free. A second later, my legs are as well.

A tiny voice within me screams for me to run. I can't. I'm too weak, though the blood is already doing its work. Katya is still stronger. She will catch me and end me, I will take the blame for this man's inevitable death, and she will kill again.

Inevitable.

He's going to die no matter what I do.

I pounce, pinning him as I feed. The power entering me is blinding, deafening. The taste of fear overwhelms everything I am until there's only darkness within me.

His heartbeat picks up its pace as it weakens, the flutter of a hummingbird trapped in a cat's jaws. I know I should release him.

I can't. The void in me expands as I take his life into myself with his blood. I groan against his throat as the flow slows. Every weakening beat of his heart makes me stronger than the one before. As strong as Katya after her kills. More powerful than I've ever been before.

I'm going over the edge.

At last.

The moment of his death takes me beyond anything I could have imagined or hoped for. A wash of bright darkness, life from death, perfect insanity for a pure, sparkling moment. I shatter completely, losing myself in his departure.

I release his body and pull away, dazed and trembling with a strength that overflows my body's capacity. The warehouse is bright and clear. My senses are perfect. I tune out the sounds of distant traffic and listen closer.

No heartbeats. No breath, though Trixie looks like she's holding hers, waiting.

I lift the hem of my t-shirt and wipe my mouth. I've made a mess, got blood everywhere. Multiple bite wounds cover my victim's neck, as though I couldn't get enough from just one. I don't remember doing that. He's lying with his eyes wide open, staring.

I feel no urge to close them.

Whatever was in me, whatever connection I had to life, is gone. I am a vampire. For the moment, I can hardly think of anything else. I don't want to remember questioning this glorious destiny I've been pushing away for so long. This is what I was born for. Not light. Not life. Not anything that my living state provided.

I am free.

"Do you see?" Trixie whispers. "Was it amazing?"

I turn my eyes slowly back to her. "It was."

Everything is as it should be. I have no idea why I fought this. A smile tugs at my lips.

Trixie giggles. "Better than anything, right?"

I stand. The soreness is gone from my body, and I'm pulsing with energy that makes me want to run laps around the warehouse.

"Are you going to end me now?" I ask Katya.

I doubt she could. Now that my perceptions are restored, I feel the lack in her. She hasn't fed since she caught me, I'm sure of it. Maybe even longer than that. She's been waiting for me to wake, keeping that captive of hers to tempt me with, confident that I would either find my end without regaining my strength, or that I would kill and understand.

I'm stronger than her.

I push that thought aside and let the good feelings wash over me again.

Katya seems amused. "That depends on you, Aviva. Do you wish to hunt the pathetic rogues on the run from justice, maintaining the secrecy of Maelstrom by my side?"

"Yes." I can picture it. Nights on the hunt, the thrill of the chase. How did I not know I needed that?

"Will you protect me above all other elders, using your gifts to serve me in exchange for what you've just had?"

"I will." Though my particular gift seems irrelevant now. I could no more feel empathy for the man at my feet than I could for the dead rat I smell rotting inside the warehouse walls. But if I have a gift, I'll find another way to access it. There's no room for doubt here. I have become myself. I'll figure out what that means later.

"Very well, then. We'll dispose of this body, figure out how to explain your return, get you moved to my team and out of this festering hole of a city." She nudges the body with her boot. "I hope you'll prove more competent than some who have joined me. Our last hunt was a disaster."

Trixie ducks her head low. "I got a little excited. But no one got away. Our secret is safe." She peers up at Kayta, eyes wide and innocent.

Katya presses her lips together, and it looks so much like Daniel's expression when he used to get annoyed with her that I don't know whether to laugh or cry. My Trixie.

Trixie blithely turns away from Katya's disapproval, slinging an arm over my shoulders with a grin. "I'll help you adjust to things. It won't be so different now, except our training will be way better."

"All will be normal for a while," Katya says. "Regular feedings will keep us well above suspicion. I think we've had enough excitement for now."

The light fades from Trixie's eyes, but only slightly. We have all the time in the world. The next thrill can wait.

God, I feel good. And it doesn't feel like this will fade like it does when my prey walks out alive and satisfied. I suppose it will go eventually, but then I'll have this again. All it will cost is a few human lives. Insignificant things.

Little things. Like Kari.

Kari, who wasn't sure she wanted to be a Black-Smith after all, because that sounded funny.

And her brother, who just wanted his Teddy and his mama.

Does that matter anymore? The lump in my throat says it does, but it can't. They shouldn't mean more to me than a veal calf does to humans. Hell, we should start raising them in tiny barns. Keep them tender.

I snort, then laugh until tears stream down my face. I don't know why. My own thoughts are horrifying me to the point where I have to either laugh or scream. Every emotion is in overdrive, and all I want is that peace I felt after I fed. This is overwhelming. I can't process it.

"Leave her alone, Trixie," Katya orders, and Trixie pulls away from me. "Let her gather herself. We need to be going."

She pulls out her phone to make a call and stalks away from us.

I stretch, letting good feelings infuse me as my thoughts fade to insignificance. The sheer bliss of killing floods through me, washing away my bad feelings, my hatred of what Katya did to those children, the regret and horror that could rip me apart for the life I just took. I don't allow any of that to exist in this moment. Joy and euphoria cover everything else I might be thinking.

Or planning.

Maybe Daniel wasn't the best trainer for me, but he did teach me a thing or two about hidden intentions.

I feel so good that Katya doesn't feel me coming until I'm almost on top of her. It's only Trixie's squeaked-out warning that makes her turn, ready to fight.

She lashes out with a punch aimed at my face, but I'm riding high on the life I just ended, and I'll be damned if I'm going to let him go to waste. Not now. I duck, dart, and come at her again. It's like a high-speed dance, the two of us striking, blocking, kicking and throwing punches. My perceptions are high, as fast as they've ever been. A human opponent's blows would seem to be coming at a tortoise's pace, but Katya has the same skills as me, and she can move just as quickly.

She has the advantage of age, centuries she's spent building her strength and skills. I'm young and inexperienced, but I just killed.

And I don't care about getting out of here anymore. I may finally have accepted what I am, but there's nothing for me in Maelstrom if I've gone rogue, no forgiveness for what I've done. I'm as good as finished anyway. All I care about now is taking Katya with me, and my desperation drives me harder than anything ever did during my training.

I slip past her defences and strike her hard in the nose, and something cracks. She yells and charges at me, unfazed, and catches me around the waist. I brace myself, but slip in a puddle of oil that's leaked from one of the boxes she knocked over. Katya tackles me to the floor. If she's studied formal fighting techniques, she's not using them. She's pissed, and this is a street fight now.

She pins my arms against the floor above my head. "Weak," she spits. "Foolish. Even now, when you've tasted eternity."

She's too strong. I arch my back and kick upward, but I can't reach her. "Am I supposed to thank you for that?"

Katya sneers and leans in closer. "You've got blood on your face, dear."

I scream and whip my head forward, smashing my forehead against her jaw as she pulls back. She curses as I push her off and squirm away. She turns, looking for something.

The box cutter lies on the floor just a few paces away. I lunge for it, but Trixie screams and stomps on my hand before I can grasp it.

Katya takes the cutter and races for a set of metal stairs.

"Viva, calm down!" Trixie cries. "It's okay! You're confused, but we can help you." She seems unsure of what she should do, and she sinks to her knees beside me, offering the comfort I've always needed from her.

I jump to my feet and kick her as hard as I can in the head. She goes down, but it won't be for long. I hate hurting her, even if she's not who I thought she was when I defended her against Daniel's suspicions. But I can't think about her now, and I can't let Katya get away. If she does, that man died for nothing. I won't be able to prove anything.

I reach the top of the stairs and slow. She's here. I can feel her.

There. Crouched across a catwalk halfway down the warehouse. Waiting.

"Don't act like you didn't enjoy it," she says, rising as I approach.

"No, I did. You weren't wrong."

She laughs, low and dangerous. "Like it or not, you're one of us. A true vampire in every sense, and a rogue. One without friends or allies to hide you. You'd better run. It won't take us long to hunt you down. Maybe I'll let Daniel do the honours. It's been so long since he had a chance to take an enemy down."

One more reason to hate her, as though I didn't have enough. I run at her. She holds her ground, weapon poised and ready. I duck, and she brings it down into my shoulder, slicing through skin and muscle. I land on her, hard. She's pinned, but I can't win like this. No matter what I do to her, she's going to recover.

You can't choke a vampire. Can't kill one with a fall, and that box cutter wouldn't take her head off even if I could get my hands on it.

I need to immobilize her, but I need to get rid of that cutter first.

She pulls it free and stabs me again, under my ribs this time, coming from behind. The pain barely registers.

When she pulls the blade free again, I grab her arm and smash it against the railing support next to my head. She grunts, and the weapon clatters to the concrete floor far below.

She shoves me hard with both hands, and I stagger back, on my feet before I can lose my balance.

"You can't win," she snarls. "Come downstairs with me. I'll give you the rest of the medicine you had before. I won't even tell Daniel what you did. You can disappear quietly."

I back away slowly, and she advances.

Just a few more steps.

There.

"Somebody's here!" Trixie calls.

Katya lunges at me as one of the big bay doors in the wall behind me rattles up, filling the space below us with blinding sunlight. Trixie screams in pain, and Katya turns at the sound. Only for a split second, but it's enough.

I grasp the chain I'd spotted hanging from the catwalk earlier, pull a length free, and twist it around her neck as I shove her off balance.

She catches herself, throws a punch at me. Instead of ducking back, I lean in, hitting her hard in the stomach with my injured shoulder. She pitches over the railing, clutching at the back of my shirt as she goes, pulling me with her.

I grab the edge of the catwalk as I go down, and rugged metal bites into the flesh of my hand. My shirt rips, and Katya falls. The chain jerks tight, suspending her between floor and ceiling. She screams as direct sunlight sears her flesh.

I'm not doing much better. I'm not exposed to the worst of the light, but it's bad enough. I feel like my skin has been doused with acid. I twist sideways and swing myself like a pendulum until I can pull myself back up to the shadows of the catwalk.

I collapse onto my hands and knees and vomit from the pain.

Blood drips through the open steel and onto the floor.

Someone far below yells. A male voice. Familiar.

God, no.

I force myself to look down.

Seven vampires enter. I know what they are by their power, if not their faces, which are shielded behind black masks with mirrored panels for them to see from. Three carry guns. I don't want to know what they're loaded with. One of the weaponless ones points at Katya. The three with guns head toward the stairs leading up to us, while the other three surround Trixie.

I could still run. But what then? Wait for them to hunt me down after I have to feed again?

I won't. Never.

But I can't starve, either.

I lace my fingers together behind my head, staying on my knees on the catwalk as one of the hunters holds a gun on Katya and another hauls her up by the chain.

The third approaches me with heavy footsteps. I close my eyes.

He grabs me by my upper arms and forces me to my feet, shoving me into the deeper shadows at the far end of the catwalk, then removes his mask.

"Daniel." Relief and regret wash out of me in the breath that carries his name. I want to fall into his arms. I can't. Katya was right. I'm the enemy now, no matter what I might have felt from him before.

"Aviva, what happened?"

I can't speak. Sobs wrack my body as my victim's terrified, staring eyes return to my mind and the full weight of my crime crashes down on me. I stopped Katya. I don't know whether it was worth the price.

"Katya's leading the rogues," I gasp. "Trixie joined them for the last hunt. They're killing for fun, for... It's a game, Daniel. A fucking game."

I collapse, and he catches me, easing me to down to sit. "I went and found evidence in Kilbride, and she caught me there. I was so hungry, so weak, and she brought me here, and—"

"Daniel!" someone calls below, from among the boxes. I don't want to look, but I do. A black-clad form drags the body out and displays the ragged wounds in his neck.

Daniel's face turns pallid. "Aviva. Did you do this?"

Katya's screaming now as she tries to shield her reddened, blistering skin from the sun. She doesn't look like an angel now. Two vampires are holding her, but she's rogue strong even if she's injured and hasn't fed in a few days. She breaks free from one. I expect a gunshot. Instead, he reaches into a pouch on his belt and uncaps a long needle that he jabs into her arm. She slumps to the catwalk floor, and they leave her where she lies.

Is that it? I knew justice was quick, but...

I'm not ready.

But I can't deny what I've done, or explain it in a way

Daniel will understand. Or more importantly, Miranda. I've protected what she built, but that doesn't change what I am now.

I hate Katya for what she forced me to do. I'm sorry that man had to die. But deep within my darkest heart, I know that I don't regret what I did. I've only begun to use up the life I stole from him, and I'm already craving more.

I've gone rogue.

"Daniel, I didn't mean to. Katya made me, but I..." I'm sobbing again, barely able to get the words out. "He made me strong, and I fought her. I *killed* him."

Daniel shifts back on his heels and looks me over. His brows knit together over his beautiful eyes. "God, Aviva."

My emotions are shifting again, toward despair as strong as the euphoria that filled me just a few minutes ago. I wipe my arm across my face, and when I pull it away my white skin is streaked with bright blood. His blood. The human I killed. Who I enjoyed killing.

My motive doesn't matter. Maybe catching Katya was an excuse to find out what I was truly made for.

I'd do it again right now if I could.

If I could...

I collapse as my mind fractures again, overwhelmed by the grief inside me. I'm only vaguely aware of Daniel calling for the medic, of hurried footsteps coming toward me, of the needle slipping into my flesh.

It's better this way.

CHAPTER NINETEEN

Awareness comes back in a rush, accompanied by light that leaves me blind. I'm pinned flat on my back on a soft surface, restraints around my wrists and ankles. I don't remember how I got here. I grunt as I struggle to sit up, and can't. I panic, yanking at my restraints.

Strong hands pin me down, two on my upper chest and more on my stomach and thighs. Someone calls for a shot, and I struggle harder. Something is very wrong. I just can't remember why.

Masked faces come into focus as my eyes adjust to faint sunlight filtering through curtains into a sterile white room.

Doctors. Vampires.

"Step back." I recognize the voice, and force myself to be still.

Daniel's tone doesn't leave any room for disagreement, but one of the doctors tries.

"She'll hurt herself, or someone else," she says, glaring at him over her shoulder. She wears mascara so thick her eyelashes look like spider legs, and for a moment they seem to be crawling. I blink hard, and the illusion disappears.

Daniel appears beside her, looking down at me. Our hair doesn't grow quickly after death, but he's got a solid five o'clock shadow going, like he hasn't been home in a while. He shoots her a dark glare that I'm glad isn't directed at me.

"I said to let her go. This is one of our finest hunters, not a common rogue. You will treat her with the respect she deserves."

The doctor gives him another hard look, but steps away. They leave, all except Daniel. He doesn't touch me, just sits on a hard plastic chair beside the bed as I try to sort things out.

I'm hungry again, craving blood, feeling dead. Not like I was when I woke up in that warehouse, but—

Oh, God. The warehouse. Trixie. The memory of fear-drenched blood coats my tongue, carrying with it a mixture of shame, disgust, and perfect bliss that I want more than I hate the other things. I force myself to remember the body on the floor, his throat torn apart.

I did that.

The craving calms, but leaves a faint tremor in my limbs.

Daniel waits, watching me.

Something else is wrong. Missing. Maybe it's just that I'm hungry, but I feel... free. Disconnected in a way that I fear even though it's quite a peaceful feeling. Like something in me has been severed.

An anchor.

I ignore Daniel's probing stare and focus within myself, sorting things out, looking for the warm scrap of whatever it was that connected me to life. A lingering shred of a soul, or whatever made me so different. So weak.

It's gone. Maybe it was never really there to begin with, and I was just clinging to the memory of it all this time. In any case, I suspect Katya was right. I'm all vampire now, just as she is, or was. And Daniel. And the others. The thought doesn't sadden me as I might have expected. Once I've placed it and named it, it's not so bad.

I'm still me. Still Aviva. But I'm connected deeply with the endless void within me. It's eternal, as I thought my soul was. It's not the same, but it is every bit as wondrous.

I am here. I am aware. I have not lost myself as I feared I would. And I suspect I still have the capacity to choose what that means.

My muscles relax, and I look to Daniel. "Where am I?"

"Medical facility. Not the same one you went to after your making."

That's good. I never want to go back there. I suspect that even when I've found complete peace with what I am now—if that ever happens—I won't want to. The negative memories are too strong.

Daniel rubs his hands over his face. He doesn't seem himself. Rougher, exhausted, and more stressed than I've ever seen him. It's like when his accent slips, but more so. His mask of composure is off. This is the Daniel he hides from everyone.

I can't say it's a bad thing.

"Am I the only patient here?"

"You are. Trixie and Katya are gone."

"Gone?"

He nods. "I didn't see either of them after we left the warehouse. Katya is an elder and will get a trial."

"Will I have to be there?"

"No. The elders deal with their own."

I don't ask about Trixie. She's as new as I am, and I doubt that Katya felt any need to protect her.

I want to cry for her, but I can't. Maybe later, when I've fed. When I'm well.

He reaches toward the floor and pulls a paper file up onto his lap. "I'm supposed to debrief you. Evidence for the trial, information to be filed for reference."

"And then what?"

He frowns and leans forward. "That depends on you, I suppose. Tell me what happened."

He's all business now. Mask back on, so very like the Daniel I've always known. If anything changed between us in recent weeks, I don't imagine it's permanent. Especially now, after what I've done. If he thought I was dangerous before, I guess I've proved it now.

It doesn't take long for me to tell him everything. We start with my issues, my shameful connection to the living, and finish with my sedation in the warehouse. He records every detail, including his own suggestion that I stop trying to break my connection to the life I left behind. I doubt that's something he really wants in a permanent record, but it's important.

I don't mention the day he spent in my bed, and he doesn't ask about it. Not important at all.

I ask whether the guys who tried to mug me can remain off-record, but he shakes his head. "It's important that the elders know. They understand what we are better than anyone, remember. They existed as vampires before Maelstrom came into being. They've felt what you have. They may have created our laws to prevent things like Katya's little game from exposing us, but..." He caps his fountain pen and puts the papers away. "We all understand the hunger, Aviva."

"So I won't be executed as a rogue?"

He leans back in the chair. "You'll have a lot of recovery time ahead of you. Sort of a detox program. And something like probation. But based on what I know of you, I've recommended that what you did in the warehouse be treated as actions taken to prevent further crimes. Means necessary to reach an end." There's almost a question there.

One that I can't answer. "Thank you," I say. It's almost a whisper.

"I'm sorry I didn't believe you."

The shock of Daniel apologizing leaves me silent for a few seconds. "You did in the end," I finally say. "You didn't let her arrest me."

His brow creases again. "I helped you escape because I didn't want to lose you, and I didn't trust her to give you another chance if she thought you were a threat. I still thought you'd come around, see how crazy your suspicions were." I stiffen at the word crazy, but don't respond. "I was trying to protect you, give you time to understand the facts."

He pulls his chair closer and leans forward. "I was wrong. I've been living within Maelstrom for a long time, abiding by its rules, accepting its beliefs. Your gift defies some of those beliefs. You're different, and our society does not reward that. Everything hinges on us respecting the system and the hierarchy." He pauses, swallows hard. "And I thought I knew Katya. We've had our differences in the past, but we've also worked together successfully. It was hard for me to consider that I could be so blind to what she was."

"Not just you."

He forces a smile. "No, she fooled everyone except you. Maybe I would have listened to you more closely if I hadn't given a shit about your safety, but I do. I was afraid you might get hurt, and it nearly ruined everything." He pulls his fingers through his thick hair. "I need to be more careful about that. You are terribly dangerous, you know."

"I guess it's natural for a trainer to be protective," I offer, and he smiles.

"That must be my problem."

"Can you untie me?" I tug at the thick velcro straps that hold my wrists. "This is quite uncomfortable."

He looks away.

The door swings open. "I heard someone is awake!" chirps a chipper young voice. A living woman in green scrubs enters, high ponytail bouncing with every enthusiastic step. "Hungry?"

"Absolutely."

"Excellent. The doctors say that if you're awake and calmed down, we can take care of that. If you feel ready, of course."

I'm beyond ready. Daniel isn't acting like he's going to leave, which is awkward. I haven't fed in front of an audience since my recovery days, long before I met Daniel. It's a private thing for me. Still, I'm hungry enough that it hardly matters.

She smiles and leans in. She smells different. There's

something strange yet familiar in her blood. Sweet, but not terribly compelling. Still, it's blood. Human blood. My mouth waters.

"Are you sure?" I ask, even as I struggle to pull myself closer in spite of the bonds that hold me to the bed.

"Absolutely. It's pretty rare that a vampire has to come to a hospital, you know. I've been just about going crazy here."

She's the perfect opposite of the man in the warehouse, not only in her physical appearance but in her attitude. Whoever she is, she's here by choice, eager to let me feed.

She positions herself carefully, bracing her hands on the bed rails. I don't need any more encouragement than that.

The skin of her neck is thick and lightly scarred, but I find a place where I can slip my fangs in with little resistance. She sighs and leans in further, and I wish I could wrap my arms around her and hold her closer still. The urge to tear her skin to open the flow of blood is nearly overpowering, but I resist. If I misbehave, she'll leave.

And I don't want this to end. Her blood is hot and good. She might be a regular at this, but she's strong, and her life flows into me as I feed. I feel her weakening, and remember the shattering moment when I took a life. It's so close I can feel it.

She pulls back, and I can't hold back the growl that rumbles from me before I regain my senses.

"Sorry," she says, and presses a gauze pad to her neck. Blood trickles from underneath, staining the edge of her top. "Just a little at a time to start. This is your rehabilitation, friend." She winks. "I look forward to next time."

I collapse back against the bed, filled with strength that tempts me to try to break the heavy straps that hold me. I feel good. But I want more.

Daniel is looking out the window. I didn't see him move. When he turns back, the apprehensive look he gives me makes me wonder whether he knows what I'm feeling. He always seemed so straitlaced, my trainer. I wonder if Katya was right, if he craves the hunt.

He sits on the bed again, but doesn't speak.

"You going to untie me now?" I ask again.

"No. After we're done talking, if you seem okay."

"There's more?"

He clears his throat. "Did you notice anything odd about the woman you just fed from?"

"She smelled different."

"Kelsey is special," he says. "She'll become one of us some day. After she dies, of course. It's a long story, but she knows about us in a way most of the living never will, and she's happy to help us while she can."

Our world is so much more complicated than I ever realized. The amount I still have to learn is overwhelming. Not just about what we are, but why.

"Daniel, Katya said that killing was our true nature. What we were created for. Do you think that's true?"

"Katya's full of shit."

But he looks away when he says it. Daniel has controlled himself for many decades, has never killed. But looking at him now, I understand that it's as hard for him as it is for anyone.

"Be that as it may, it makes me wonder," I say. "Who made us, and why?"

He sighs. "I don't know, Aviva. There are stories, but I suspect that's all they are. I'm not sure we'd like the answers if we sought them. We fill a niche in the supernatural world. Maybe that's all there is to it." But he doesn't sound sure.

I want to sit up. This is pissing me off. I feel weak when I'm restrained.

"I guess I don't have to know about a great purpose," I add as I tug at the bonds. "I'd settle for getting my hands on my file and finding out who made me."

Daniel was reaching for the velcro, but he stops and rests his hand on the bedrail. "Why? So you can hurt him? Tell him how miserable you are, how you wish he'd left you to become fully dead and see what was on the other side?"

My breath catches. "You know who did it, don't you?"

As our eyes meet, I think I know, too.

He brushes his fingers over mine, just barely, and sits again without releasing me. "It was the stupidest thing I've ever done. We were on assignment halfway across the country, following a band of rogues. True rogues, you understand, not like Katya's. We'd hunted them down and finished them, and we celebrated. I was still feeling good the next night and decided to go for a walk. And I saw you." He smiles at the memory. "You looked like trouble. I'd passed the party in the woods and was walking toward you as you charged down the street. We almost bumped into each other."

A chill cuts through my horrid hospital gown, prickling the hair on my arms. "I don't remember that at all."

"The anger was baking off of you. I could practically smell it, along with your blood factor. I was bored, and more than a little curious. There weren't any living people in your area who were marked for potential change. So I followed you to see what was going on."

My stomach feels empty in spite of my recent feed, like a cold pit. "You just watched him kill me?"

"I'm sorry, Aviva. I truly am." He sounds like he means it, and my anger fades, if only a little. But I still can't really comprehend what he's saying. "As you said, it happened quickly. And I wasn't about to reveal myself for the sake of a living person who got herself in a bad situation. But I did go to you before the paramedics got there. After your sister realized you were dead and ran away."

Ouch. I may no longer feel connected to my life as I once did, but that hurts.

"You were dead, but not completely gone. There's a window of time where we can make a vampire after death, but I knew it would be lost if the paramedics came and took you." His eyes seem distant, like they're looking all the way back to that night. "And I knew I should just leave you. I don't quite know, even now, why I didn't. Maybe it was because we'd just finished the rogues, and the executions were so final. There was nothing else for them, and I wondered whether your blood factor meant the same for you. It seemed unfair."

He makes a face like the word tastes bad.

"I took you. Carried your body through the woods and back to the motel where we were all staying. Laid you out on my bed." He raises his eyes to meet mine. "Which is not as creepy as it sounds, I promise."

I don't smile at that. "Go on."

"Not much more to tell. I did a stupid thing. I made you, though you weren't marked for it. I knew that meant you were unsuited. But I'd seen the determination in you, felt the passion of your anger, and I couldn't let that slip out of the world when I could save you."

I've never looked at it as being saved. Strange. "And that's why you were demoted?"

He laughs bitterly. "It is, indeed. There were other punishments before that, but somehow it was okay. I knew they wouldn't try to end you once you were made any more than a doctor will kill a new baby, no matter how ill-suited it is to its new life. It was the stupidest, least-rational decision I've ever made, and I wasn't a bit sorry for it."

"Was it horrible?"

He grimaces, and I can't help smiling. "Disgusting. My advice is never to try it. I really thought drinking that much dead blood was going to be the end of me. It was every good feeling from a feeding turned on its head, as low as the highs ever reach. I was lucky you'd already lost so much from your wound, but still. It made me so damned weak. Then before you woke, Katya found us. She had the others take you to the facility with orders that no one should ever know who had done this terrible thing. And then she returned and made me understand the serious-ness of the situation."

I'm not going to ask about that. Heavy silence weighs the room down.

"Was I worth it?"

He smiles slowly, perhaps surprised that I'm not reacting with anger. I'm surprised, too. I think any other answer would have reopened my wounds, but I can't be angry at Daniel. Whether what he did was right isn't important. It's done. I'm here. And my near-execution made me realize how glad I am of that. I'm not ready for this to be over.

"So far, I suppose you have been. Mostly." He looks me over. "I mean, you've been a pain in the ass since I picked you up again at the facility like a lost puppy. But you're not so bad."

I stick my tongue out at him and he laughs. It sounds as relieved as it does amused.

"Not angry, then?" he asks.

"Untie me and we'll find out."

He touches my fingers again, more firmly, and traces his way up my arm to the sensitive skin above my elbow. I shiver. He leans in close, so that his lips brush the edge of my ear. "I think I like you like this," he murmurs. "Helpless for once. Completely at my mercy."

"Daniel..." I'm impressed I can sound this angry when I'm quite the opposite. Hunger stirs in me that has nothing to do with feeding. I'm relieved to find that his effect on me hasn't changed. I really am still myself. Maybe more than I was before.

He sighs and stands up, then reaches for the straps. "Very well."

It feels good to have my hands free. As soon as he unshackles my ankles, I cross my legs and sit up to stretch.

"Does that mean you don't hate me for what I did, then?" I ask. "For any of this?"

"No, I don't. I was terrified for you until I sorted things out with Miranda and got the hunt headed in the right direction. And I hated that feeling, but I've never hated you."

I rub the kinks out of my wrists. "What changed your mind?"

"I was never entirely sure, to be honest, until we entered that warehouse and found the three of you. But when Katya made an excuse for having to leave town with Trixie, I decided to see where your suspicions took me." He seems as uncomfortable with this as he does with the memory of his decision to turn me.

"How did you find her?"

He smiles sadly. "Trixie had many gifts, but awareness of her own visibility was never one of them. We tracked her, not Katya."

Had. That's it, then. She made her choice, as I made mine. Same crime. Different motivations. Different consequences.

"Miranda's really going to let this slide?" I ask.

"Assuming the elders accept the story as you've given it today. It will remain in your record, but you won't be tried or executed. As I said, we all understand." He bites the edge of his lip. "To be honest, I'm a little jealous. It's probably best if you don't tell me what it was like."

I want to touch him. I want his arms around me, and I want to know that whatever weird thing we're building between us isn't destroyed.

"I should get my notes back to Miranda," he says, reaching for the leather bag I can now see on the floor beside his chair. "Do try to behave yourself while I'm gone."

"I'm insulted."

He snorts. "You're trouble. But that's not the worst thing."

I think for a second that he's going to lean in and kiss me, but the spider-eyed doctor enters the room. Daniel nods to her, and then he's gone.

CHAPTER TWENTY

D aniel returns the next day. I haven't fed again, but I'm still feeling pretty good. There's not much here to stress me out. Katya is taken care of, and the living of St. John's are safe enough for now, completely unaware of the world that lurks beneath the surface of their beautiful city. I'm safe here, too, and I've had time to think.

I'm ready to take my place in Maelstrom. Whether my peculiar gift remains now that my connection to life has been severed, I don't know. I suppose I won't unless I stumble on another body, and I don't know when that might happen. I'm guessing there's a good chance I'll be moved now, trained in a position that allows a bit more oversight until I prove myself trustworthy. And that's okay. I can accept it for a time, knowing that it's not forever.

I've meditated, or tried to. There's no light in me that I

can focus on, and even the desire to pray to anything like light or a creator seems to be gone. That saddens me more than I'm willing to admit even to myself, but there's relief there, too. I'm whole now, no longer torn between worlds.

When Daniel enters the room, it's with a tight smile. He's slept, showered, and shaved, but he looks less all-business than he did last time. That's good.

I hope.

He's got that bag with him again, and it sounds heavy when it hits the floor.

"I have an assignment for you," he says.

"Does that mean I'm officially pardoned?"

He smiles, if only halfway. "It does. You're to get out and make yourself useful as soon as you're cleared to leave here. But not as a hunter. Not for a while. The elders want you in a..." He hesitates. "Quieter position."

He doesn't say anything more, but looks uncomfortable.

"What?"

"You're not going to like it."

"Damn it, Daniel. Just tell me. Rip off the bandage in one go if it's that bad."

He reaches into his bag and pulls out a map, then sits on the bed as I unfold the paper.

Newfoundland. Gros Morne National Park is a pink blotch on the west coast, its borders highlighted in yellow. A red star marks an inland space just to the east of the park's borders, far from any marked roads. I hold it closer to my face to examine the tiny letters printed there.

"You're joking."

"Not at all. Aviva, you need to be away from the living for a while, just until the elders are sure you've recovered. And they need someone to help supervise the werewolf sanctuary." He shrugs, apparently having little else to offer. "At least you'll be busy. And you'll have time to do some reading. You're cleared for whatever library materials you want. Basic training is officially over, and your security clearance is... well, bottom level, but that's better than before."

I groan and look at the map again. This was the assignment Daniel used to threaten us with if we didn't shape up and prove ourselves worthy to work with him. He's right. There are no communities close enough to tempt a vampire with rogue tendencies, except one.

"Bloody Bight?"

"Small community, isolated. Willing to take a chance on having our kind nearby. We move stock in and out as necessary, but otherwise there's not a lot of traffic other than the most intrepid explorers from outside. Your situation will complicate things, but you'll be able to handle it. I have complete faith in you."

I trace the highway from the sanctuary back to St. John's. It has to be an eight hour trip, maybe more. "How long will I have to be there?"

"I don't know. Months, at least. A year. The vampires who are doing it now have been there for decades, but I don't think you'll stay that long. Maybe you'll love it. At least you won't have to deal with the kind of excitement we've had around here recently, right?"

I imagine breaking up fights between wolves who think they're all alpha males and doubt it will be much of an improvement. "I need a coffee. Maybe something stronger."

"So you'll go?"

As if I have a choice. "I'll go where I have to. What's a year, right?" I force a smile. I haven't been around long enough for years to seem like a short span of time, especially when I'll be spending them alone or with strangers. My throat tightens. "I, um... I can't say I won't miss you. Will I ever see you if we're not working together?"

He presses his lips together. "If you want, absolutely. Actually, I was going to ask whether you might want company for the journey."

I'd swear my heart skipped at his words. I let out a sharp laugh. "You want to come to the werewolf sanctuary?"

"Not at all. But I'd like to at least see you settled, if you'll have me."

I open myself to him. I may have lost the key to my strange gift, but I still have this. I feel something from him, faint but true. He's uncertain about all of this, but he's not any more ready to let go of me than I am of him. It feels a little strange now, knowing that he made me, realizing how much I owe him. But it doesn't change anything.

I'm not supposed to care for him. But I do.

I give him my most inviting smile. "I guess that might not be so bad."

He leans over the bed and presses his lips to mine. Hesitant. Certain he shouldn't be doing this.

But then, I guess I already have a habit of making him do things he knows are wrong.

The map falls to the floor as I wrap my arms around his neck and pull him closer.

This might not be forever, but for this moment, it's everything.

The End

NOTE FROM THE AUTHOR

Thank you for purchasing this book! I hope you've enjoyed reading it as much as I did writing it. I look forward to sharing what comes next with you. If you liked this one, Sanctuary is going to blow your socks off.

If you enjoyed Resurrection and have a few moments to tell your friends about it or leave a review, I'd certainly appreciate it. Spreading the word on books readers love is what keeps authors in business and able to produce quality books at a pace that leaves you not wanting to murder us.

Well, most of us. Not speaking for everyone.

For news on upcoming releases, giveaways, advance reading opportunities, stories, and other awesome stuff, visit www.tanithfrost.com and click the newsletter tab to sign up. You'll be the first to learn about what's next in the Immortal Soulless world... and whatever comes next.

-T.F.

ACKNOWLEDGMENTS

This book has been in the works for a long time, since the Easter Sunday evening when a vampire whispered in my ear saying she had a story to share. Though she's had to wait a few years to see it finished, I hope she's pleased.

Thanks to this long process, I owe gratitude to a lot of people.

To the brave readers who tackled the earliest, novella-length draft and encouraged me to keep going, thank you. AM Leibowitz, KL Schwengel, Shannon Andrews... I hope you still recognize the parts you loved, and that everything else is only better.

To my revised version critique goddesses, Krista Walsh, Shannon Andrews, and Laura Fischer, thanks for the kind words and brilliant suggestions. And to my lovely beta readers, Kathy Dunlavey, Kristina Sprague, and Shannon Martin, thank you for spotting the stuff I screwed up. Annnnnd for not laughing at me too much over it. Extra special thanks to Nadine Smith for not only reading, but for checking my Newfoundland references. (Any mistakes are of course mine, not hers.)

To my editor, Sue Archer, big thanks as always for fitting me in, respecting my voice, and making my words the best they can be.

And thank you to Jessica Allain for the gorgeous cover art.

Thanks to my alter ego's street team, this book got to have a wonderful crew of volunteer proofreaders. Annette Flick, Mary Medina, Per M Jensen, Sharon Eastridge, Hetal Patel, Percy Ledbetter, Margie Scheiner, Charlotte Sandberg, Sarah Husch, and KL Schwengel's eyes (and enthusiasm) were all very much appreciated.

To my family, thank you for respecting my space and my need for these flights of fancy, for your excitement, and for putting up with take-out so often when deadlines got tight. I love you guys.

-TF

ABOUT THE AUTHOR

Tanith Frost lives somewhere in central Newfoundland. She deeply resents having to share her time, office, and brain space with another author who INSISTS on writing other shit and taking care of her family and stuff. So unreasonable. Her interests include reading, writing, and avoiding the general public at all costs.

She does, however, grudgingly admit that hanging out with people on social media isn't so bad. So if you're looking for her, here's where to find her:

www.tanithfrost.com

ALSO BY TANITH FROST

THE IMMORTAL SOULLESS SERIES

Resurrection

Sanctuary

Atonement

Covenant (June 2018)

Temptation (coming soon)

More titles to be announced

visit www.tanithfrost.com for details on upcoming releases or to
sign up for the author's newsletter